Sven Grundtvig, Jens Christian Bay

Danish Fairy and Folk Tales

A Collection of Popular Stories and Fairy Tales

Sven Grundtvig, Jens Christian Bay

Danish Fairy and Folk Tales
A Collection of Popular Stories and Fairy Tales

ISBN/EAN: 9783744693813

Printed in Europe, USA, Canada, Australia, Japan

Cover: Foto ©Andreas Hilbeck / pixelio.de

More available books at **www.hansebooks.com**

"HE PAID NO ATTENTION TO HER TEARS AND PRAYERS"

Danish Fairy & Folk Tales

A Collection of Popular Stories and
Fairy Tales. From the Danish of
Svend Grundtvig, E. T. Kristensen
Ingvor Bondesen, and L. Budde

By

J. Christian Bay

Profusely Illustrated

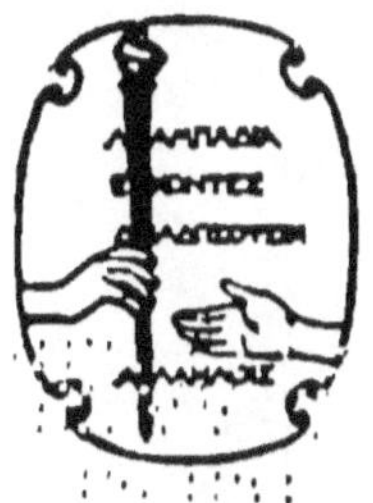

NEW YORK AND LONDON
HARPER & BROTHERS PUBLISHERS

TO

HELMUTH OLE CHRISTIAN BAY

FATHER'S OWN BOY

WHO ALWAYS LIKED A " MAOUW-BOOK "

PREFACE

HE fairy tales and popular stories gathered in this volume are "Danish" only insomuch as they have been collected among the population of Denmark, and are colored by the thinking and doing of the people of this country. It would be difficult, indeed, to apply the name of any nationality to any of the numerous popular stories gathered by a host of ardent and studious collectors in the different European countries. Very few of all these tales can be truthfully said to have originated in the native land of those into whose spiritual life they have entered.

The framework of all genuine European fairy and folk tales are of Indo-European origin. The stories have spread from one country to another, and from one individual to another, without losing their original typical character; they have become disseminated among the population by means of *living words*—words which sound and are heard—which breathe into the listening ear the glee and woe of the hero; the sorrows of the faithful against whom foul play is started, and the many insignificant yet collectively important details and incidents that produce the obligate tears or smiles.

Whether told in the Jutlander's broken dialect, the singing tone of the " Fynboer," or in the Zealander's rolling provincialism, these tales are built upon the same foundation, and become adapted, through sympathies roused, or indignation called forth, to the receptive powers of the listeners with which the story-teller is always familiar. Thus the form in which we receive a story from some old woman, or nurse, depends in a certain measure upon the ways and habits of the population which has preserved the tale. At the same time, the ingenuity and the memory of the narrator are important factors in producing the dramatic or moral tenor appreciated by the listener. Hence the same story may be found in Denmark, Germany, Servia, or England, comprising the same facts and founded upon one common "plot," with the exception of certain details; but the mode of telling, the tinge of nationality or of individual peculiarities—these are as different as the momentous charm produced in telling.

The folk tales of the Danes are prominently illustrative of the ways and habits of this nation. Interwoven as they are with the best and brightest thoughts, hopes, and aspirations of " the plain people"—the rural population—they cannot but repre-

PREFACE

sent certain essential features of popular belief and aspiration. They are never better understood than when told by an old farmer in his frieze coat, "tasselled cap of red," and wooden shoes with straw in the bottom. In fact, there is no better means of communication from man to man than the living word.

May this train of Danish kings and queens, wise men and fools, princes and beggars, peasants and burghers, soldiers, fairies, and trolls — may they all be kindly welcomed by our American boys and girls!

The sources from which most of these stories were gathered are principally the works of the late Professor Svend Grundtvig, one of the most conscientious Danish folk-lore students. In addition thereto, the collections of E. Tang-Kristensen, Ingvor Bondesen, and Molbech have been consulted. The writings of Budde, Jens Kamp, and a few others have supplied a few tales, and in a few cases personal memories were called to assistance.

Mrs. Dora Bay, my wife, and Miss Mary Whitcomb, of the Iowa State Historical Department, have given me much good advice, for which I am truly grateful.

J. C. B.

CONTENTS

CONTENTS

ILLUSTRATIONS

ILLUSTRATIONS

DANISH FAIRY AND FOLK TALES

DANISH FAIRY AND FOLK TALES

A ROSE-LEAF

AD the fountain of speech dried up, or why did silence prevail in the High Council of Babylon?

There they were, seated in a circle, all the wise fathers of the great city; all were ab-sorbed in deep meditation, fixing their glances upon the ground as if expecting that help and advice would grow up, like herbs and flowers.

What had brought the High Council of Babylon into such a state of helplessness and confusion? It was a small slip of parchment upon which were written these words: "*Abdul Kader asks Babylon to show him hospitality.*"

Abdul Kader—the light of the Orient, the wisest among wise men—whose speech was vivifying as balsam, refreshing as rain. He asked Babylon to open its gates for him—Babylon. the city of thou-

A

sands, numbering already hundreds of thousands. Were he admitted, ten would follow, and hundreds would follow the ten, and thousands would follow the hundreds.

But the worthy man must not be treated like an unwelcome beggar. He could not be refused admittance! And yet—

Suddenly the doors were opened, and Soleiman, the Elder, entered the hall. The marks of wisdom were written by age upon his forehead.

When he saw the lines written upon the slip of parchment he remained standing in the middle of the hall. Every one gazed at him, but a long time elapsed; then a ray of light gleamed from his eyes, and seizing a costly cup, he said to the Council, "Arise, and follow me."

They all followed him to the fountain near the gate of the city. Here Soleiman filled the cup with water, and when it was unable to hold another drop, he lifted it, and with a kind smile, but without speaking, held the golden chalice towards Abdul Kader, as if wishing to say: Behold! Babylon is like this cup which cannot hold another drop of water; Babylon has not room for another man.

But Abdul Kader smilingly reached down, picked a rose-leaf from the ground, and cautiously placed it on the surface of the water in the cup. He spoke not, but Soleiman extended his hands towards him, and the Council forming a procession, conducted him to the hall. Abdul Kader had solved the problem.

A wise man is like the rose-leaf on the water. The leaf floats on the surface without exerting any pressure; the wise man is no source of trouble to a community. He beautifies it

HERE was once a king who lived far, far away in a country the name of which no one knows. He had an only daughter, who was of so sad and melancholy a disposition that no one remembered having ever seen her smile. She was now a grown girl, pretty and good, but always sorrowful and downcast; if she did not weep she was melancholy, and showed such low spirits that it seemed utterly impossible for any one to cheer or to gladden her.

The king was of a very amiable disposition, and indeed a very able man to manage his country; but the condition of his daughter caused him such deep distress and anxiety that he became gloomy and was out of humor. He had only this one child, and she would, of course, inherit the kingdom when he died. She looked so downcast, however, that he feared she might suffer an early and untimely death.

The king consequently made known throughout the land that he who could win a smile from the princess would be honored with her hand in marriage and ascend the throne with her when he, himself, died. There were many who came and tried their best, but no one could even make her smile. They only succeeded in making twofold fools of themselves, first, when they attempted to amuse her, and, second, when they were obliged to return home with a long face—disappointed.

His majesty grew tired of witnessing all their endeavor: both the merriment he had to look at and the jokes to which he must listen wearied him; but he was disappointed, especially, when he looked at his daughter, who remained as gloomy and sour-faced as before, in spite of all their pranks and jokes. A new order was now given to the effect that those who came and tried, without success, to make the princess laugh, should be dipped in tar, rolled in feathers, and sent away in disgrace. This edict lessened the number of contestants, but the princess remained as downhearted as before.

In the same land there lived a man who had three sons; the eldest was called Peter, the second Paul, and the youngest Saucy Jesper. They lived a quiet, secluded life, hence a long time passed before they learned of the king's edict, and how easily their fortunes were made if they could win a laugh from the princess. Peter thought he might as well do his best, and try. His mother gave him a good knapsack, and his father a purse filled with money. Thus equipped, he started on his journey.

On his way he met an old woman who drew a

small sledge after her. She stopped and asked him for a bite of bread and a penny. Peter answered, however, that he had no more of each than he would need in the long voyage before him. "Your voyage may be an unhappy one," said the woman. But Peter did not listen to her; he went on, announced himself at the royal palace, and was ushered into the presence of the king and the princess. He now began singing the funniest songs ever heard —this was the art in which he trusted—and one after another he sang the most amusing airs, but with no effect; the princess remained gloomy as ever. Peter was accordingly dipped in tar, rolled in feathers, and dismissed from the palace. His mother used a whole barrel of butter in removing all the tar from him.

If Peter did not succeed, Paul might have better fortune, at least he thought so, and wished to try. He, too, received a good-sized knapsack and a purse; and he, too, met the old woman, who asked for a bite of bread and a penny. But as he also refused to help her, she left him saying that his journey might not bring him happiness. When Paul was called into the presence of the king and the princess, he tried *his* art, which was to tell the funniest stories anybody had ever heard, and with which he had amused many other persons. He did his best; both he and the king laughed heartily, but the princess only yawned. So he met Peter's fate and returned home in a miserable condition.

Saucy Jesper was not frightened by the awful fate of his two brothers, but declared he would start on the same errand. "What are you thinking of!" said his parents. "How can you imagine that you will ever succeed when both of your brothers failed? And yet they are better men than you. They know songs and stories, and you know nothing but how to make such a fool of yourself that one can both laugh and cry over it."

"To laugh is sufficient," said Jesper. As no amount of reasoning would move him, and as he was determined to go, his mother gave him a piece of dry bread, and his father one penny, whereupon he left with no one's blessing.

When he had walked a while, and needed rest, he seated himself at the road-side and began eating his dry bread. While he was thus engaged, an old woman came along the road, drawing a small sledge after her. She stopped and begged for a bite of bread and a penny. Jesper at once gave her what remained of his bread, and his one penny.

"Whither are you going?" asked the woman.

"To the king's palace. I think I can make the princess laugh, and then I shall marry her," answered Jesper.

"How will you do it?" continued the woman.

Jesper said he did not know, but hoped he would get an idea.

"I think I can help you," said the woman, "since you helped me. You may have my sledge—

you will notice there is a little bird carved on the back. When you seat yourself in it, and say 'Pip, little bird!' it will drive along, until you cry stop. When any one touches the sledge the bird will say 'Pip.' If then you call 'Hold on!' they must remain where they are until you bid them 'Let go!' Be careful that no one shall steal your vehicle, and I think you will be successful."

Jesper thanked her kindly for the good gift, seated himself in the sledge, said "Pip, little bird!" and was at once carried as swiftly along the road as if drawn by a pair of the best horses. All who saw it became so astonished that they nearly dropped nose and mouth from surprise. Jesper did not care, however; he drove straight onward until evening, when he stopped at an inn to rest for the night. He tied the sledge to his bed in order to prevent its being stolen. But the people at the inn having seen him arrive were, of course, very curious to know more about the remarkable vehicle. Late at night, when everybody thought he was asleep, one of the servant-girls, anxious to examine the wonderful sledge, stole slyly into the room. But as soon as she touched the sledge the bird said "Pip!" "Hold on!" commanded Jesper, and there the girl stood, unable to tear herself loose. Soon another girl stole into the room and took hold of the sledge. "Pip!" cried the bird again. "Hold on!" shouted Jesper. There were three servant-girls at the inn, all equally curious, so at length the third one came

"THE WONDERFUL PROCESSION"

in and was caught like the rest. There all three
stood.

Early in the morning, before any one was up,
Jesper took his sledge into the court-yard, the girls,
of course, following. Appearing not to see or hear
them, he took his seat, saying "Pip, little bird!"
and the sledge immediately began to move on as
the day before. The girls, who were not prepared
for such an event, ran as fast as they could, and you
may be sure that they had a most excellent exer-
cise at this early hour of the day.

After a while they passed a church. It so happened that the minister and the sexton were about
to walk in ; but when they became aware of the
singular procession, they stopped and gazed at it in
great astonishment. The minister became angry
and called to the girls to stop. As they did not
obey him, he ran after them and tried to hold them
back. " Pip !" said the bird. " Hold on !" added
Jesper, and the minister was obliged to follow, run
ning at the top of his speed. The sexton, who saw
this, and considered it his duty to assist the minister, ran after them and caught hold of the reverend
gentleman's coat-tails. " Pip !" " Hold on !" said
Jesper again, and the poor sexton was forced to
dance along with the rest.

They soon reached a blacksmith-shop, the owner
of which was standing near the road with a pair of
tongs in one hand, and in the other one some hay
he was reaching to a horse which he had just been

shoeing. This blacksmith was a merry fellow, and when the procession passed him he burst into laughing and reached for the sexton with his tongs. "Pip!" said the bird. "Hold on!" cried Jesper ; and the blacksmith was, himself, forced to fall in line.

Some geese came walking slowly along. When they saw the hay in the blacksmith's hand, they could not afford to miss the opportunity, but rushed after and snapped at it. They could not tear themselves loose again, however, but were obliged to join the parade.

Very soon Jesper and his followers arrived at the palace, and passing through the gate, in great speed, drove three times around the court-yard. The girls wept and cried ; the minister and the sexton panted and yelled ; the blacksmith laughed and swore, and the geese quacked and hissed. The whole court came out and looked at this wonderful procession. The king laughed until the tears stood in his eyes, and when he turned around—behold! there the princess was standing, laughing as if she would never stop, and wiping the tears from her eyes with her handkerchief.

"Stop!" cried Jesper. The sledge obeyed. "Let go!" was the next command. The geese, the blacksmith, the sexton, the minister, and the girls immediately disappeared in different directions.

But Jesper skipped up-stairs to the princess. "Now you are cured," said he, "and now you are mine!" And thus it came to pass that Saucy Jesper came into possession of the princess and the kingdom.

THE COFFEE-MILL WHICH GRINDS SALT

HERE was once a little boy by the name of Hans. As his parents died while he was very young, his grandmother took care of him and taught him reading and writing, and to be a good boy. When she became very old, and thought she was about to die, she called the little boy to her and said: " I am old, Hans, and may not live long. You were always a good boy, and therefore you shall have my only treasure, a coffee-mill which I have always kept at the bottom of my old chest. This coffee-mill will grind all that you wish. If you say to it, 'Grind a house, little mill,' it will work away, and there the house will stand. When you say, 'Stop, little mill,' it will cease to grind."

Hans thanked his grandmother kindly, and when she died, and he was alone in the world, he opened the chest, took the coffee-mill, and went out into the world. When he had walked a long distance, and needed something to eat, he placed the mill on the grass and said, "Grind some bread and butter, little mill." Very soon Hans had all that he needed, and then he bid the mill to stop.

The next day he came to a large seaport, and when he saw the many vessels, he thought it would be pleasant to see more of the great world. He therefore boarded one of the ships and offered his service to the sailors. As it just happened that the captain needed a boy of Hans's age, he told him to stay.

As soon as the ship was out of port, the sailors commenced abusing Hans. He bore the harsh treatment as well as he could, and when he had nothing to eat the mill ground all that he wished. The bad men wondered how he could always be contented, although they gave him but little to eat. One day one of them peeped through a hole in the cabin - door and discovered how the coffee - mill served him. Now the sailors offered a large sum of money to Hans if he would sell his treasure. He refused, however, saying that it was all that his good old grandmother had left him. So one day these wicked men threw Hans overboard and seized the mill. As they were in need of some salt, they bid it grind for them. The mill immediately began its work, and soon they had enough. Now they asked it to stop, but as the one who had peeped through the hole into the boy's cabin had not learned the exact command, the mill refused to obey, and before long the ship was filled with salt. The men grew desperate, but none of them was

able to find a way out of the difficulty. So at
length the ship sank down with the mill, the salt,
and all the wicked men. The men were drowned,
but the mill is yet standing at the bottom of the
sea, grinding away, and for this reason the water
in the ocean has and always will have a salt taste.

HERE was once a merchant whose business was so immense that he was the wealthiest tradesman known. He had three daughters, one of whom was named Beauty. One day the merchant received word from friends far away, informing him of the failure of one of his connections, and he at once prepared himself for a journey to that place. The two older daughters asked him to buy all sorts of finery and dresses for them, but Beauty asked for nothing at all. When the merchant left, these two girls had rubbed their eyes with onions in order to look as if they were sorry to bid him good-bye ; but Beauty needed no such artifice ; her tears were quite natural.

So the merchant went away, and in due time arrived at the place where the tradesman of whom he had heard the bad news was living. But instead of obtaining money, as he hoped, he was kicked and beaten so violently that it seems a great wonder he came away without losing his life. Of course he had now nothing to do but return, so he mounted his horse and turned homeward. Towards evening he unfortunately lost his way, and when it became quite dark he knew no better than to ride in the direction of a light which was shining from a distance. At length he reached a beautiful little palace, but although it was lighted, there seemed to be no one at home. After a while he found a shelter and food for his horse — pure oats, and nothing else. The animal might well dance for joy, for both man and beast were wellnigh exhausted from the long ride. When the horse had been provided for, the master stepped into the palace. There a light was burning, and a table was laid for one person, but no one was to be seen. As the merchant was tired, he sat down without invitation, and ate a hearty supper. A fine bed was there, too, and when he had eaten enough he stretched himself among the pillows and enjoyed a good night's rest.

The next morning everything appeared as on the evening before. The horse was well supplied, and as breakfast was ready on the table, the merchant seated himself, doing justice to the good meal. As he was now ready to leave, he thought it might be well to look over the premises, and glancing into the garden he perceived some exquisite flowers. He went down, intending to carry some of them home with him as a present for Beauty; but no sooner had he touched them than a horse came running towards him as fast as it could trot, saying : "You thoughtless man ; I was good to you last night, I gave you shelter and provisions, and now you would even take with you the most beautiful flowers in my garden."

The merchant immediately begged pardon, saying that he had intended the flowers as a gift for Beauty, his daughter.

"Have you several daughters?" asked the horse.

"Yes, I have three, and Beauty is the youngest one," he replied.

"Now you must promise me," said the horse, "that you will give me the daughter whose name is Beauty; if you refuse, I will take your life."

Well, the merchant did not wish to lose his life, so he promised to bring his daughter to the palace, whereupon the horse disappeared among the trees, and the man rode home.

As soon as he reached his house, the two older daughters came out and asked him for the fine things which they were expecting. But Beauty came and bid him welcome. He produced the flowers and gave them to her, saying, "These are for you, but they cost your life;" and he then told her how he had been obliged to make the fatal promise to the horse, in order to save his life. Beauty at once said, "I am willing to follow you, father, and am always glad to help you." They started on their journey, and soon arrived at the palace.

As before, no one was to be seen, but the merchant found food for his horses and a good stable

The table was also laid for two persons, and there were two beds. Having done justice to the supper, father and daughter retired and slept soundly. When they awoke the next morning, they found breakfast ready for both, ate heartily, and having exchanged many loving and tender words, they separated, the father riding away. We will let him proceed, and see what occurred at the palace.

Shortly before dinner-time the horse arrived. He came into the room and said, "Welcome, Beauty!" She did not feel very glad, and had all she could do in keeping her tears back. "You shall do nothing but walk around in these rooms and in the garden," continued the horse. "Your meals are provided for. I shall come home every day at noon; at other times you must not expect me."

Time passed, and Beauty felt so lonely that she often longed for noon, when the horse came home, and she could talk with him. She gradually came to look at him more and more kindly; but one thing caused her great distress, namely, that she had no news from her father. One day she mentioned this to the horse.

"Yes," said he, "I understand that very well. In the large room you will find a mirror in which you can see all that you are thinking of."

She was happy to learn this, and went straight into the room where the mirror was hanging. As soon as she thought of her father, her old home was visible in the glass, and she noticed how he was sitting in his chair with a sorrowful expression upon his countenance, while his two daughters were singing and dancing. Beauty felt sorry over this state of affairs, and the next day she told the horse what she had seen.

"Your father is sorry, I suppose," said the horse, "because he has lost you. He will soon feel better, however."

But on the next day, when Beauty consulted the mirror, her father looked pale and ill, like one who is deadly sick; both of her sisters were dressed for a ball, and neither of them seemed to care for the weak man. Beauty burst into tears, and when the horse came home, asking what ailed her, she told him of the bad state of affairs, wishing that he would allow her to return and nurse her poor father during his illness.

"If you will promise to come back," said the horse, "you may return and stay for three days; but under no condition must you break your word."

Beauty told him she would come back in three days.

"To-night," resumed the horse, "before going to bed, you must place the mirror under your pillow, saying: 'I wish to be home to-morrow.' Then your wish will be fulfilled. When you desire to return, you must do likewise."

The next morning, when Beauty awoke, she was at her old home. Her father became so glad to see

"A BEAUTIFUL YOUNG PRINCE STOOD BEFORE HER"

her again that he at once felt a great deal better. She cared so well for him that the next day he was able to be up, and on the third day he was almost well. As he wished her to stay with him a few days longer, she complied, thinking that no harm would come from it. On the third day after, however, when she looked into the mirror, she saw the horse stretched on the ground in front of the bench which was her favorite seat in the garden. She now felt that it would be impossible for her to remain longer, hence in the evening, before going to bed, she placed the mirror under her pillow, saying: "I wish to be at the palace to-morrow morning."

She promptly awoke in the palace the following morning, and hurrying into the garden she found the horse so very sick that he could not stand on his legs. Beauty knelt down and asked him to forgive her for staying away longer than she had promised. The horse asked her if she could not persuade herself to stay with him all her life, but she answered that it would seem very singular to live with a horse all her lifetime. The poor animal now sighed so deeply that she took pity on him and said, fearing that he might die then and there, that she would always stay with him and never leave him. As soon as she had made this promise, the horse vanished, and a beautiful young prince stood before her. He seized her hand and asked whether she was not sorry for the promise she had made. No, she said, she would rather stay with him now than when he was in the shape of a horse. He now told her that both he and the whole land had been enchanted by his wicked step-mother, who had converted him into a horse, and told him that only when a beautiful young girl would promise to stay with him, in his altered shape, would the enchantment be over. He wanted to marry Beauty, and live in the palace which belonged to him.

So they sent for her father to take up his residence with them, and now the marriage was performed and celebrated in a splendid manner. They lived long and happily together, the prince and his Beauty.

NCE there was a wealthy miller who lived near the high-road. Above his door he had written these words: "Here lives a man who is free from sorrows and trouble." One day the king, happening to pass the house, stopped and read the inscription. "I shall give him trouble," thought he, and having ordered the miller to appear before him, he gave him three questions to be answered to the king's satisfaction within three days. If he failed to answer the questions, he must forfeit his life.

As the miller walked about in the fields pondering on this difficult problem, his shepherd asked what grieved him, since he looked so troubled. "It is of no use to tell you," answered the miller, "for you cannot help me." "Yes," said the shepherd, "if you will only tell me all about it, I am ready to help you." So the miller told him all. "Oh, is it not worse?" exclaimed the shepherd. "If I may borrow your clothes, I will answer the questions for you."

On the appointed day the king returned, and the shepherd received him in the miller's clothes.

The first question was: "How long will it take me to make a voyage around the world?" "May I take time to consider?" asked the shepherd. The time was granted him, and in a little while he said: "If your Majesty follow the sun, it will take only twenty-four hours." "That is well enough," said the king, "but can you tell me how much I am worth in my full equipment?" The shepherd answered: "Our Saviour was sold for thirty pieces of silver, therefore your Majesty cannot be worth more than twenty-nine." This answer was also well received; but at last the king said: "Now I shall ask the third question, and you must have no time for consideration. Can you tell me what I am thinking?" "Yes," replied the shepherd; "your Majesty thinks you are speaking to the miller; but I am only his shepherd."

The king at once declared himself satisfied, and the miller escaped further trouble.

MANY years ago an old soldier was discharged from the army. He received in consideration of his excellent and faithful service a small loaf of rye - bread and three pennies, whereupon he was at liberty to go whither he pleased. As he was walking along the high-road, he met three men; the one carried a shovel, the second a pickaxe, and the third a spade. The soldier stopped, looked at them, and said, "Where are you going?" "I will tell you," answered one of them. "To-day there was buried a man who owed each of us one penny, and now we will dig him up, since we are determined upon getting our dues." "What an idea!" returned the soldier; "you had better leave the dead man alone. At any rate, he is at present unable to pay you even one penny, so don't disturb his peace!" "It is all very fine for you to talk," answered the man; "but we must have the money, and up he must come."

When the soldier felt that his fair words could not settle the matter, he said, "Here, I have two pennies; will you take them and promise to leave the dead man undisturbed?" "Two pennies are not to be refused," said the man again, "but they will pay only two of us. What can you give the third one, since he is bent upon having his share?"

As the soldier saw that there was no dealing with these three wretches, he resumed: "Since you are so desperately determined, here is my third and last penny. Take it, and be content." Now all three were well satisfied, so they pursued their way with the three pennies in their pockets.

When the soldier had advanced a distance, a stranger came walking along. He looked rather pale, but saluted the soldier in a very civil manner, and followed him along the road without uttering a single sound. At last they reached a church, and here the stranger turned to his companion, saying, "Let us walk in!" The soldier looked wistfully at him, and answered : "That would not do. What business have we in the church at midnight?" "I tell you," replied the stranger, "we must walk in!" Upon this they entered the church and walked straight up to the altar. There was an old woman sitting with a burning light in her hand. "Take a hair from her head, and smell at it!" commanded the stranger. The soldier complied, but nothing remarkable happened. The stranger asked him to repeat the action, which he did ; but there was no effect. The third time, however, when he tore a whole tuft of hair from the woman's head, she became so furious that she darted off, out above

the church, carrying the whole leaden vault with
her.

The two men went out of the church and down
to the beach, where they found the whole leaden
vault. Turning to the soldier, the stranger said,
"Sit up; we will put to sea!" "Is that so?" remarked the soldier, who understood nothing of all
this. "I see no ship, however." "Let me manage
it all," says the stranger; "just seat yourself by me
on the vault! Beyond the sea there is a princess
of whom it was predicted that she would be married
only to a man who should come across the sea in a
leaden ship. Here you will be able to make your
fortune." The leaden vault now floated out upon
the open sea, and landed them safely on the other
side. Great was the joy and happiness throughout
the country, and the marriage between the soldier
and the princess was celebrated with such pomp
and splendor as was never seen, before or after.

When the ceremony had been performed, and the
carriage was standing in front of the church door,
bride and groom entered, with the stranger who
had followed the soldier all along. The coachman
asked to what place he might drive them. "Drive
away, as fast as you can, towards the side where the
sun will rise," said the stranger, and in a little while
they were carried along at a furious rate. Somewhere they saw a large herd of cattle. They stopped,
and the soldier called the herdsman to the carriage
door, asking who he was. "I am the Count of Ra-

vensburg," answered the shepherd, "and yonder is my castle." The stranger again bid the coachman drive as fast as possible. In a little while they rushed up to Ravensburg Castle. As they were ready to alight from the carriage, there was some one who knocked hard at the gate. It was the herdsman, who was anxious to come in. The stranger walked to the gate, inquiring what he could do for him. He wished to come into the castle, he said, for it belonged to him, and he had a right to demand admittance. The stranger meditated a little, whereupon he told the herdsman—who was a conjurer—that he might be allowed to come in, but first he must suffer the whole fate of the rye. "The fate of the rye!" repeated the conjurer; "what do you mean by that?" "I mean," answered the stranger, "that next fall you must be sown deep in the ground, and towards spring, when you come up, you must ripen in the sunshine and grow in the rain until you are ready for the harvest. Then you will be mowed and dried, and kept in the barn, until at length you will be threshed." "How is that!" cried the conjurer; "am I to be threshed?" "Of course you are," replied the stranger. "First you will be threshed, and then taken to the mill and ground." "Ground, too!" shouted the conjurer; "will I be ground also?" "Yes, both ground and sifted," answered the stranger. But the conjurer, hearing this, became so furious that he burst all into flint-stones.

"'I AM THE COUNT OF RAVENSBURG'"

THE THREE PENNIES

The stranger now bid good-bye to the princess and the soldier, shook hands with them, and said : "Now I have seen you married to the princess ; the troll of Ravensburg is dead and gone, and his castle, with all its treasures, is yours. I was as good to you as you were to me when you gave away your three pennies for my sake !" "What do you say ?" exclaimed the soldier ; "I never thought of those three pennies again !" "I know that," answered the stranger, "and otherwise I would not have been able to help you. However, I bid farewell to you and your wife, for I must return to the place where I belong."

THE LITTLE MARE

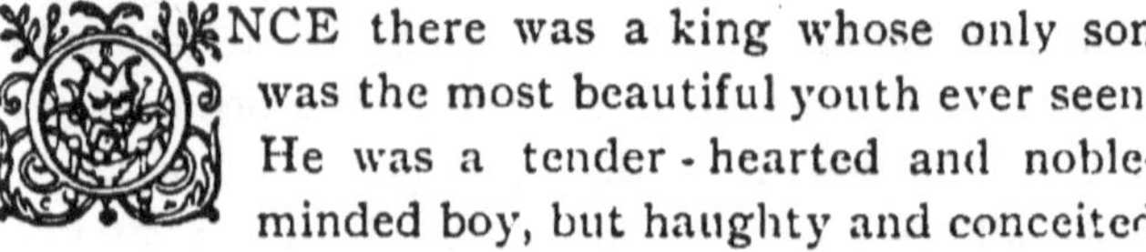

NCE there was a king whose only son was the most beautiful youth ever seen. He was a tender - hearted and noble-minded boy, but haughty and conceited on account of his rank, his beauty and accomplishments. As he was himself handsome, he liked all that was fair and graceful, but hated anything ugly or hideous; he would always say that he grew sick when looking at what was displeasing to his eyes.

It happened one day, when he went hunting with his comrades, and the party was camping near the high-road to enjoy a good breakfast, that they noticed an old man who came along the road riding a miserable mare. This old man was very unpleasant to look at, as he was hump-backed and one-eyed, had a crooked neck, and of course was poorly dressed. The mare was not prettier than her rider; she was a small, fleshy, long-haired jade, lame in one fore-leg.

"Pooh," said the prince, "get that ugly old fellow and his hideous mare out of the way. I cannot endure the sight of anything so shocking." The courtiers were at once ready to obey him, and soon the shabby rider and his horse were driven out of the prince's sight.

The old man was not, however, what he appeared to be, but a great and mighty conjurer, who did not always present himself in such a wretched shape. One day when the prince was walking alone in the woods, the old man suddenly stood before him and, touching him with his staff, said: "Now you try and see what it is to be a mare like mine, and that you shall be until an innocent young princess calls you her dearest friend." The moment he had uttered these words, the prince was transformed into just such an ugly little mare as the one which he could not bear to look at.

At the home of the prince every one was alarmed at his disappearance, and no one knew what had become of him. In the mean time he walked about in the woods as a common little mare, not at all satisfied with himself. He knew it would be useless for him to return to his father's palace, as no one would know or care for him. When he had been walking about in the forest for a couple of days, a little boy who gathered wood happened to see him, and approaching him he patted his back and talked kindly to him. The little mare followed the boy wherever he went, and finally they came to the boy's home just outside of the forest.

"Look, father," said the boy, "here I bring us a new horse instead of the old one which died yesterday,'

"That is a poor bargain," answered his father; "this one is an utterly miserable animal. It is hardly worth its feed; but we will try it, anyway." So the little mare was put in the stable, and the next day, when the man hitched her to his plough, he found that she served him well. "She works better than she looks," said he to Hans—this was the boy's name; "you must feed her well; in course of time she may prove a great help." Hans thought a great deal of his little mare, as he called her; he curried and fed her with great care, and treated her kindly. Of course she was obliged to work for her food; but towards spring, when the fields had all been tilled, the farmer said to his son: "To-morrow you may go to town with the mare and have two of her hoofs shoed, for now I will sell her."

Hans was not pleased with this, for he would rather keep his little mare. When he came to town and had her two hoofs shoed a one-eyed man came walking along, fell into talk with him, and at length asked if he would sell the animal. "Two hundred dollars is the price," answered Hans, jokingly. "That is too much for her," said the man; "but well and good, I will pay it." "No," said Hans again, "she does not belong to me; she is the property of my father, and I have no permission to sell her." "Then you may go home and ask permission," said the man. Hans declined, however; he mounted and rode home, but did not

"THE SHABBY RIDER AND HIS HORSE"

mention to his father the offer of the two hundred dollars which had been made him.

Shortly afterwards there was a horse-market in town, and the farmer now said to his son: "Go and make the mare look pretty; I wish to take her to the market." Hans was very sorry, and asked his father if he would not allow him to take the mare to the market. His father, however, desired to go himself. "Then father must ask three hundred dollars for her," said Hans. "You must be mad, boy," answered his father; "I know myself the value of the horse. She is not worth even one hundred dollars." Now Hans told that some one had made him an offer of two hundred. "Then you are a great fool," said his father, giving him a good box on his ear. He mounted the mare and rode away to the market-place. He was thinking, however, of what Hans had said, and when any one inquired how much he asked for the mare, he answered, briskly: "Three hundred dollars." The buyers laughed at him and said that was a large price for such an old jade, worth not even one hundred. The farmer did not lower the price, however, and at length an old one-eyed man came up to him; he did not haggle about the price, but paid it at once and took the mare. The farmer went home, and was well pleased with the profit he had made. Hans wept, however, and was very sorry The next morning, when his father looked for him, he was not to be found. "He has run after the mare," said Hans's mother, and thus they satisfied themselves.

Hans had, indeed, run after his little mare. In town he succeeded in finding out that the man who had bought her had gone with her to a place a hundred miles away. He was thought to be a rich and a great man, and presumably he belonged somewhere at the king's palace. Hans at once started on his long journey, and finally had all the hundred miles behind him. He went straight to the king's palace, and applied for a place as groom. This was granted him, but the mare was not to be found in the king's stables.

One day Hans found a small carriage out in the court-yard, and what should be attached to it but his own dear little mare. He was of course delighted to find her again, and patted and talked kindly to her. It so happened that at the same moment the king's youngest daughter—as yet a mere child—came running past; when she saw Hans standing by the little mare she came up to him and said: "Such a little pet I would like to have; I could use it both for riding and driving. Don't you think so, Hans?" Yes, Hans was quite certain; he told her that he knew the animal to be the swiftest and most pleasant in existence. The little princess skipped up to her father and asked him to buy the mare for her. "That ugly little beast!" said the king; "no, there are enough pretty horses in my stable, and you may select for yourself the one you like best." She had taken such a fancy to the mare, however, that she went on begging and praying, until the king assented and bought the animal for her. "Now take good care of her, Hans," said the little princess. Hans readily promised, and kept his word so well that every day the little mare grew more and more beautiful. The princess drove with and rode on her, and liked her very much.

Some time afterwards the king's oldest daughter —for he had two daughters and no sons—had been fishing in a pond in the garden. She happened to lose a ring which had belonged to her mother, and as it was both a great treasure and a talisman, she and her father were alike unhappy over her misfortune. The king ordered a careful search for it, but all were unsuccessful. At last the king proclaimed that he who could find the ring could be married to the princess and be endowed with one-half of the kingdom. Many princes and noblemen from this and other countries came and searched, but no one found the ring, although several actually lost their lives by exercising too much zeal.

In the mean time the little princess liked her mare better and better every day; she both kissed and patted it, and had it shoed with splendid gold shoes.

One day, when Hans was watering the little mare by the pond, he noticed a beautiful goldfish in the water, and at once jumped for it, without, however, succeeding in catching it. But a couple of days after, when he again watered the mare, she kicked the same goldfish to the shore. Hans seized the fish and brought it to the king's kitchen, where every one was anxious to see it. When it was cut open the missing ring rolled out. Then the king said to his oldest daughter: "Well, now, you will have to marry Hans!" She was willing enough, and so was Hans; but, he said, the honor was really due rather to the little mare which had kicked the fish ashore with her hoof.

When the little princess heard this she skipped down to the stable, folded her arms around the mare's neck, kissed her, and said: "No, you shall not be married to my sister, she may take Hans; but I am going to keep you always, for *you are my dearest friend.*" As soon as she had uttered these words the mare was gone, and she was embracing a beautiful young prince. He thanked her, and told her all about his punishment, and how he had now been set free. Afterwards they walked up to the king, and their marriage was celebrated on the same day when Hans was united with the other princess.

The beautiful prince went home to his father with his bride, and his return caused great happiness throughout the land. He is no more haughty or conceited, but noble and good, and happy with his little princess. Hans is also happy with *his* princess, and is now in possession of the *whole* kingdom, the old king having died.

 HERE was once a king of England whose daughter was very famous. She was the most beautiful princess ever seen or heard of. But she had one great fault—namely, that she was haughty and proud. Of course she had many suitors, but all were refused, and as she possessed a sharp tongue, she moreover scorned them, giving nicknames to every one who was bold enough to woo her.

At that time there was a young prince in Denmark. The fame of her beauty had reached him, and he sent word, asking for her hand in marriage. The princess answered, however, that she would rather earn her bread by spinning all her life than marry such a poor and miserable prince. The messengers were obliged to return with this unfavorable response.

The young prince had determined, however, that he would win her. He despatched fresh messengers with letters, and sent her a gift consisting of six beautiful horses, white as milk, with pink muzzles, gold shoes, and scarlet rugs. Such horses had never been seen in England before, hence the king put in a good word for the Danish prince: He who could send such a gift of betrothal must by all means be considered her equal. But the beautiful princess ordered the grooms to cut off the manes and tails of the six steeds, to soil them with dirt, and turn them over to the messengers, whom she instructed to tell the prince that rather than be married to him would she sit in the street and sell earthen-ware.

When the messengers returned, relating all that the princess had said and done, the Danish king became so incensed that he wanted to put to sea with all his ships and revenge this insult. His son asked him, however, to desist from any such action; he wished to attempt once more, by fair means. If he were unsuccessful, he would himself know how to take revenge. To this his father assented.

The prince now built a ship, so beautiful and costly that its like had never been. The gunwale was artistically carved with all sorts of animals; deer, dragons, and lions were seen jumping about, and the stem and stern were richly gilded. The masts were mounted with gold, the sails made of silk, every second canvas being red, and the remainder white. This ship was manned with the handsomest lads in the country, and the prince gave them a letter to the king of England and his proud daughter, the princess, asking her to accept him, and receive the ship as his gift of betrothment.

The gorgeous ship rapidly crossed the sea and stopped immediately outside of the royal palace. It commanded general attention, no one having seen such a magnificent vessel before. The couriers landed and delivered their message. Now the king used his best efforts to persuade his daughter: A suitor so wealthy and munificent, so true and devoted as this prince, certainly deserved a favorable answer.

The princess graciously listened to his entreaties, feigning an intention to·think the matter over until the next day. But at night she gave orders to sink the ship, and in the morning she told the couriers to return as best they could; that she would rather beg her food at the doors than call their poor fellow of a Danish prince her husband.

The couriers returned to Denmark with this disdainful answer, and with the tidings of the fate of the king's ship, which was now, with its gilded masts and its silken sails, at the bottom of the sea. Upon hearing this, the king at once determined to man his fleet and take a bloody revenge. The prince dissuaded him, however, vowing solemnly that he would make the haughty princess repent the disdain with which she had treated him.

Upon this he left Denmark quite alone, and reached England, no one knowing him. Disguised, as he was, in an old hat, dingy clothes, and wooden shoes, he arrived at the palace towards evening and asked the herdsman for a bite of bread and a couch.

He obtained both, and during the night kept company with the cows in the stable. The next morning the beggar—Greyfoot, so he called himself—
sought and obtained permission to help in driving
the cattle to their watering-place. The latter happened to be situated exactly outside of the windows
occupied by the princess. Greyfoot now opened a
bundle which he had brought with him, and produced a golden spindle which he proceeded to use
in driving forth the cows. The princess, who was
standing at one of the windows, saw the spindle,
and taking at once a great fancy to it, she sent
some one down to inquire whether the beggar were
willing to sell it. Greyfoot answered that he did
not care to sell it for money; the price he asked
was permission to sleep outside of her door the
following night. No, said the princess; she could
not think of such a price. "Very well," answered
Greyfoot; "that settles the matter, and I keep my
spindle." The princess had taken it into her head,
however, that she must possess the beggar's treasure,
but as she did not like any one to know that such
a poor-looking man was admitted to the palace, she
sent a secret message by one of her maids, telling
him to come late at night, and to be gone early in
the morning. This he did.

When the princess looked out of the window the
next morning, she noticed Greyfoot chasing the
cows with a golden reel, and at once sent one of
her maids down to inquire whether it could be

" THE COURIERS LANDED AND DELIVERED THEIR MESSAGE"

bought. "Yes," said Greyfoot, "and the price is the same as yesterday." When the princess heard this she was not a little astonished by the audacity of the beggar, but as the treasure could be obtained in no other way, she assented, and everything passed as on the previous night.

The third morning Greyfoot drove the cattle to the watering-place, as usual, but this time he was using a weaver's shuttle of pure gold. She sent for him, and when he appeared in her presence she said: "Now, Greyfoot, how much do you ask for *this* treasure of yours? Will you take a hundred dollars for it?" "No," answered Greyfoot, "it cannot be bought for money. If you will permit me to sleep inside the door of your room to-night, you may have it." "I think you are mad," said the princess. "No, I cannot hear of any such price. But I am willing to pay you two hundred dollars." "No," said Greyfoot again; "it must be as I say: If you want the shuttle, you must pay the price which I ask. Otherwise, I will keep the treasure myself."

The princess looked at her maids, and they looked back at her, and all looked at the magnificent shuttle. She *must* possess it, whispered the maids; they would sit in a circle around her, keeping guard the whole night. Finally the princess told Greyfoot that he might come late at night; they would let him in. He must be careful, however, and tell no one, since they were all running a great risk. When it grew late, and the princess was about to fall asleep, the maids were all sitting around her, each one holding a lighted candle in her hands. Greyfoot entered, and quietly stretched himself on a rug near the door. But as the maids were not accustomed to much waking, one by one they became drowsy, and very soon every one in the room was soundly asleep. As the ladies had rested little during the two previous nights, it was no wonder that the sun did not wake them very early the next morning.

The king, who was accustomed to see his daughter at the breakfast-table, became alarmed when she did not appear as usual, and hastened to her rooms. Imagine his surprise when he found, outside of her door, an old hat and a pair of well-worn wooden shoes. Opening the door quietly, he stole into the room. There the princess was, fast asleep, with all her maids; and so was Greyfoot, on the rug inside the door. Usually the king was a very amicable and quiet man, but when this spectacle met his eyes he became angry. He controlled himself, however, and called his daughter's name aloud. She awoke, and so did the maids, who at once escaped in all directions. But the king turned to his daughter and said: " I now see what kind of company you prefer, and although it is in my power to let this fellow hang and have you buried alive, I will allow you to keep each other. The minister shall unite you in marriage, whereupon you will both be

"'DEAR GREYFOOT, DO NOT WALK SO FAST!'"

sent away. I will never bear the sight of you
again." The king left them, and shortly afterwards
the minister appeared with two witnesses. The
haughty princess was married to Greyfoot, the
beggar; then the couple were at liberty to go
whither they desired.

When they passed the barn-door Greyfoot turned
to the princess, saying: "We cannot walk on the high-
road in this style; you must change your clothes before we depart!" So they paid a visit to the herdsman's wife, who gave the princess—now Greyfoot's
wife—a gown of linsey-woolsey, a woollen jacket, a
cape, and a pair of heavy shoes. "That fits better,"
said Greyfoot, and they walked away.

At first they walked each on his own side of the
road, without speaking; but in a little while the
princess raised her eyes to look at the man who
was now her rightful husband. To her astonishment she observed that he was neither old nor
ugly, but really a handsome young man, in spite of
his old and dingy clothes. Being not accustomed
to walk very far, especially with such heavy foot-
wear, the princess soon felt exhausted, and said:
"Dear Greyfoot, do not walk so fast!" "No," he
returned, "as I have now been burdened with you,
I suppose I cannot leave you on the open road."
So he entered the next house and hired an old
carriage, the bottom of which was covered with
straw. They now drove on, until at length they
arrived at a seaport. Greyfoot immediately sought

and obtained passage for himself and his wife, as servants, and the princess felt much relieved when at last they were out of her father's domains, although she had no idea of their destination.

The voyage ended in Denmark, and when they had safely landed, Greyfoot proceeded to rent a small hut in the neighborhood of the royal palace. It consisted of only one little room with a stone floor and an open fireplace, where she must prepare their frugal meals. In a little while Greyfoot went out, and returned with an old spinning-wheel and a large bundle of tow, of the meanest quality. "While you work with this," he said, "I must try to find some occupation, as best I can. Neither of us can afford to be idle."

Thus time passed slowly and quietly. Greyfoot had secured work at the palace as a wood-cutter, and returned every evening with a loaf of bread and a few pennies. His wife was spinning until her finger-tips were scorched, and her knees shaking under her. One evening Greyfoot brought home a wheelbarrow filled with earthen-ware. This he had bought on credit, he said, and she was in duty bound to go to town the next day and sell the things. She of course made no objections. The next day Greyfoot went to his work, as usual, and his wife set out for the town with her earthen-ware. But when she had just managed to sell a few of them, a troop of stately knights came galloping down the street. One of the horses became wild

THE MISFORTUNE OF THE PRINCESS

and rushed in among her articles, which went into a thousand pieces under the heavy hoofs which trampled upon them. The riders pursued their way; but the poor princess returned to the hut, and, sitting down, wept bitterly.

In the evening, when Greyfoot returned, she told him of her misfortune. "Now we are utterly unfortunate," said he, "for I have no money with which to pay for these articles. You will now have to sew a wallet, go from door to door, and beg for victuals and pennies, until our debts have been paid." The princess did as he bid her, and was glad that her husband did not scold her for her ill fortune. She begged at every one's door, bringing home, at length, several pieces of bread and some pennies.

"That will not bring us very far," said Greyfoot, when the princess had displayed the contents of the wallet. "I have now found a good place for you at the palace. They are preparing for a wedding, and to-morrow you are to lend a hand in the kitchen. Do your best and make yourself useful; maybe they will keep you and pay you good wages. To-morrow you will obtain your meals and twenty pennies."

The next morning, before Greyfoot's wife went away, her husband said: "To-day I must stay at home; I have felt an illness coming upon me, so I will rest and try to get better." She burst into tears, and told him that when he was ill she could not think of leaving him. When he answered, however, that she was expected, and necessarily must go, she kissed him good-bye, hoping that he would soon feel better, and promising to return as speedily as possible.

"The haughty princess" spent the whole day among the pots and pans in the royal kitchen. When she returned to the hut, Greyfoot told her that he felt better, and further related how an order had been issued announcing that the Prince of Denmark was to be married to a Russian princess. Her costly bridal-gown had arrived, but the princess herself, having been detained by wind and waves, was unable to arrive in due time for the ceremony, and on the following day every girl and woman was to present herself at the palace and be measured. She who filled the measure would be selected as the bride's deputy. "And you," concluded Greyfoot, "you must put in an appearance. If you are fortunate, your wages may be sufficient for paying our debts."

In the morning Greyfoot declared that he felt worse than on the day before, but would not keep her from going. She hesitated, but as he insisted, she threw her arms around him, kissed him, and left.

The royal measurer was busy among the many women assembled in the court-yard, and it seemed impossible to find any one who was the right measure. But when at length he reached Greyfoot's wife, he declared that she was the very person they wanted.

Now she was taken into the palace, and attired in the gorgeous gown, the bridal veil, and a pair of exquisite slippers. When finally the crown was placed on her head, every one declared that the *real* princess could hardly be prettier. In a little while a beautiful carriage drawn by six milk-white horses was seen at the door, and Greyfoot's wife was asked to enter. The prince was already seated in the carriage; she had never seen him, but remembered having heard of him in past days.

They drove along the road until they came to Greyfoot's hut. Seeing already at a distance that it was afire, the poor woman in the carriage uttered a piercing shriek, and cried: "My husband! save him, for Heaven's sake! He was ill when I left him, and may not have escaped." The prince now spoke to her for the first time, and said: "If that ugly wood-cutter is your husband, you had better leave him; he is no husband for you." But she answered: "He is my husband, and was always good and kind to me. How could I leave him? Even if you offered me the place which I am now occupying for your real bride, I would refuse it, and gladly return to the hut where I have lived the happiest part of my life!"

The prince smilingly answered: "You *are* my real bride, and kept your word when you said that rather than marry me would you earn your bread by spinning, or by selling earthen-ware, or beg for it at the doors."

Now she recognized him, and throwing her arms around him, she said that her sufferings had been of great benefit to her, and that she would now stay with him forever.

Thus " the haughty princess of England " became queen of Denmark. This happened so long ago, however, that hardly any one remembers having seen her. But the story is true, nevertheless.

THE MASTER FOOL.

HERE once lived a woman who had a very foolish boy. One day, when she had been churning, the lad wished to go to town and sell the butter. His mother objected to this, saying it would not do at all, as he had never been in town before ; but as he coaxed and pleaded for her permission, she at last consented, gave him a roll of butter, whereupon he went away.

The boy trudged along, and finally reached a large stone. Supposing this stone to be the town, he addressed it very politely, asking if it cared to buy some butter. Of course the stone made no reply. "I'll tell you," said the boy, "that my butter is of a good quality. If you wish, you may have a taste of it." Without waiting for permission, he smeared a bit of butter on the stone, and as it was a very warm day, it melted in the heat. Thinking that the stone—or the town—ate it with delight, the boy resumed : " I observe that you seem to like it. You may as well buy the whole, and I am willing to wait for the money until to-morrow." So he smeared the rest of the butter on the stone, and returned home. His mother at once asked him who had bought the butter, and what price he had received for it. "I sold it to the town and gave him credit until to-morrow," answered the boy. "How so?" pursued his mother. "You sold it to the town, you say? Why, that's nonsense. I would like to know to whom in town you sold it!" "Well," returned the lad, "I tell you that I sold it to the town, just as you told me to do." "All right, then," observed his mother; "we got rid of the butter, anyway. It was, of course, foolish to let you have it."

Next day the boy wanted to go and collect the money. His mother declared that it would be of no use: she knew he would secure nothing. But he would not listen to her; he went on his own accord, and arrived at the stone. "I have come," said he, "to collect the money for the butter you bought of me yesterday." The stone did not utter a single word, however. Now the boy became angry. "You wretch!" cried he; "yesterday you bought my butter, and to-day you refuse to pay for it—nay, even to answer me. Upon my word, I will show you that I am not to be trifled with." Thus he took hold of the stone and struggled with it until it tipped over, whereupon he found that it had covered a pot filled with money. Not hesitating for a moment, he picked it up and returned home with it.

When the woman saw her son return with so much money, she was greatly astonished, and proceeded to ask him where and how he had procured it. "I obtained it from the town, mother," answered he. "At first it refused both to pay and even to answer, so I grew angry, turned it over, and took all its money. I was sure, all the time, that it had enough to pay with; but it was stubborn, and did not wish to pay." "I don't comprehend your foolish talk," answered his mother. "How could you overthrow the town? Never mind, however; you realized a great deal of money."

Some time passed, and the woman slaughtered her cow. The boy wished to take the meat to town and sell it; so a large piece was put into a basket, with which he started off. This time he really came to town. When he had walked about the streets for a while, he met several dogs which barked at him. "How do you do!" said the boy. "Do you wish to buy some meat?" The dogs barked again. "Very well," answered our friend; "you may taste it." The dogs at once began to eat it. "Take all of it, then," said he, throwing the remainder before them; "to-morrow I will come for the money."

Next morning he returned and found the dogs in the street. Having saluted them, he told them that he had come for the money. The dogs barked and barked, but produced no money. "What!" cried he; "do you refuse to pay me? Indeed, I will teach you manners." As one small dog carried a pretty collar, he considered it one of the prominent members of the party, and seizing it, placed it under his arm, saying: "I see that you refuse to pay what you owe me; but I will teach you something else before we part. Depend upon that!" Having delivered this speech, he repaired to the king's palace, the dog under his arm.

The king had a daughter who was very beautiful, but always downcast and afflicted. Her father had declared that he who was able to cheer her and make her laugh would be at liberty to marry her and ascend the throne with her when he himself died.

When the boy arrived at the palace one of the sentinels stopped him, forbidding him to pass. "How?" exclaimed the boy. "Am I not permitted to seek my rights by the king, when I am being cheated by villains? What a confounded state of affairs!" "What is your errand, then?" inquired the sentinel. The boy proceeded to tell him all, whereupon he was allowed to pass on condition of promising to pay the sentinel one-half of the money for the meat. Soon he was stopped by another guard, who also made him promise to pay one-half of the money which he hoped to obtain. At length he reached the king's rooms, and his presence was announced. When the king appeared the boy told him how wrongly he had been treated. The king

merely shrugged his shoulders, and said : "If you
have sold the meat to the dogs you must see how
you can obtain your money. I cannot help you
collect it." "Well," said the boy to the dog,
catching hold of his collar and giving him a thorough shaking. "you are a good specimen, aren't
you ?"

Upon this the king's daughter, who had listened
to the whole story, was unable to keep herself from
laughing. "Now you may secure a good price for
your meat," said the king to the lad, "for you are
free to marry my daughter." "No, I don't care for
her," answered he. "You don't !" said the king ;
"well and good, I will give you a sum of money,
for really I would rather that you should not marry
her." "Money I don't care for," declared the boy.
"If money cannot satisfy you," inquired the king,
"what *do* you wish?" "I wish sixty raps of bastinado for my meat," declared the boy. " You shall
have them," answered the king, "although that
seems a poor reward." "Come here," continued he,
turning to his men, "and give this boy sixty raps
of bastinado." "No, thank you," said he ; "the
sentinels must receive them ; they forced me to
promise each of them one-half of the payment for
the meat." Thus the guardsmen received their
dues. "Listen to me !" now said the king. "I am
sure that you are not so foolish as you seem. Will
you not marry my daughter?" "Yes, I will," answered the boy ; "since the soldiers have received

what was due to them, and are entitled to no more."
He was accordingly married to the princess, and
they lived long and happily together. It seems
to me that this was well done by such a foolish
boy!

WHAT THE CHRISTMAS STAR SEES

I

UNDER THE ANGEL'S WINGS

ON the dim twilight a young mother sits by the window. Her little son, her only one, is on her lap. It is so charming to sit quietly in a corner near the window, while darkness gently settles about you, and watch the stars rise from the deep shadows in the sky, glittering forth, one by one.

She clasps her arms fondly around her little boy, and says, softly: "Look, how all the small stars smile and twinkle at us. They have something to tell."

"What is it, mama?" asks her little boy. His mother continues:

"'We are but very small spots,' say the stars to you and to me, 'of all the splendor within the sky. But soon Christmas comes with the child Jesus, and to him it all belongs. He sends an angel through the darkness, with gifts for all his children below. The angel keeps them under his wings,

He will give you all that you wish for, that you may know how well Jesus loves you.'"

"Does he love you, too, mama?" asks the little boy. She nods.

"And papa?"

"Yes," she says, drawing a long breath, "he loves him so well that neither papa nor I really know *how* well."

"That was my testimonial!" exclaims a merry voice behind them — papa's voice. They had not seen him enter the room. "Well, what do you wish, little one? Wish, wish, while it is time!"

The little boy meditates and seems irresolute. On a sudden he looks smilingly into their faces, and says: "First, I must find my place under the angel's wings."

"He knows how to wish for plenty, the little fellow!" exclaims his father. "He wants all at once."

"Look!" ejaculates the boy, pointing to the sky. A light is kindled there. Slowly, in a wide, gleaming circle, it shoots across the firmament, and disappears within it.

"A shooting-star! Your wish will be fulfilled, my own boy," says his mother, clasping the child more tightly in her arms, while he claps his hands delightedly.

"Have it; have it all!" merrily resumes his father. "But you must be sure and return home. Do not let the angel fly away with you! I would not lose you for all the wealth of heaven, my little boy."

"Oh, do not say it in such a manner," exclaims his wife, pressing her hand against her heart in sudden alarm; "you make me so afraid."

"My pious little wife!" answers he; "how can these foolish shooting-stars frighten you? Now I leave you for my work, and in the mean time you may cherish your hopes about divine things. A mother does this all the better when she is alone."

With moistened eyes she turns towards him, whispering: "I wish both of us could do it."

"I am more easily contented than both of you," he returns, smiling upon her; "I shall not ask for heaven, but am contented with the earth, where I have you and the boy."

Kissing his two dear ones, he leaves them. A young man, with all the joy in life yet before him, he is so wise and self-reliant, so strong and good, too.

But mother sits alone with her little son. One shooting-star falls after another, and for every one of them she takes him more firmly in her arms.

Another evening: Christmas night.

The young mother again sits alone with her little boy, her only one, on her lap. It is sad to sit with such a treasure in your arms, while the darkness settles about you — it is sad to watch the glowing cheeks and the eyes which sparkle, not from a yearn-

ing or glee, but because the violent coughing takes
his breath away and shakes the little body. Mother
folds her quivering hands around the glowing forehead. Father is sitting immovable, watching his
child.

Healthy and fresh, with rosy cheeks, did he fall
asleep the previous evening; hot and feverish did
he awake in the morning. The Christmas joy vanished, giving room for the shadows of anxiety which
fell upon the home. The physician came and went
during the day; now he is expected back.

Suddenly the coughing stops, a gleam of relief
spreading upon the child's countenance. He re-
covers his breath and turns to his mother, whispering:

"Mama! Will I find my place under the angel's
wings to-night?" This was his thought and longing
for many days and weeks. But mother can only
nod; she dares not venture to answer the question.

"Mama, kiss me! Papa, come here!"

His mother bends over him, and his father kisses
the little face. There is a happy smile, a faint
struggle, and a deep silence at last.

In the room, where stood a Christmas-tree which
will not be lighted, sits the young mother, alone.
The door is opened, and her husband walks softly
in. Bending over her, he looks into her tearless eyes.

"The shooting-star," he says, at length, "spoke
the truth. Your boy and mine is now under the
angel's wings. We both believe it, you and I."

She feels that she is alone no more.

A feeble ray from the Christmas star reaches the sorrow as well as the joy. Its blessed light comes from the little figure under the angel's wings.

II

A CHRISTMAS GIFT

We are in the large city. The clocks show that it is late in the afternoon. The streets are crowded with people who all know that the following night is Christmas Eve, and are anxious not to be late on any account.

Straight through the crowds a little boy and girl, brother and sister, are rushing along, closely followed by a big dog and a small puppy. The latter is really rolling along rather than trudging with the rest of the company. When there seems to be danger ahead, the big dog snatches her offspring from the ground, carrying the little ball-like creature in her mouth, until the number of rapidly moving feet diminishes, and the passage becomes less dangerous. This little company of four is as busy as if some one's life depended upon its movements, and such is, indeed, the case.

The big dog's name is Ada, and she is doomed to be hanged. The puppy has no name; but he will be drowned.

Ada had developed of late two rather disagreeable habits. One of these is that she is always abundantly well supplied with puppies. Although she does not mean to give any one trouble with her large family, the latter surely gives her considerable cause for worry. Mama says that the puppies are dirty little fellows, and papa declares that there is no end of bother on their account. At length he becomes impatient, and in his extreme annoyance declares that in the afternoon Ada must be hanged. and the puppy drowned. No pleading or coaxing helped this time, as had been the case before; papa would not listen; he was too seriously annoyed.

What a great sorrow had descended upon the children to darken the bright Christmas Day! For over an hour they were crying over the poor puppy and his dear mother, upon whose soft pelt their little heads had often rested. But, suddenly, John is struck by an idea. Lifting his head from the soft pillow he dries his eyes, and says: " I know, sister, what we must do. We will make somebody a Christmas present of Ada and the dear puppy. I never heard that anybody was allowed to hang or drown their Christmas gifts."

Emma assented at once, whereupon all four started on their expedition. They determined to go first to Aunt Lizzie, who was so tender and good.

" Here we are, Aunt Lizzie!" they cried, when at length they were confronted by this lady; " here is

Ada and the puppy. We are going to make you a Christmas present of them, Aunt Lizzie!"

"God forbid!" exclaimed Aunt Lizzie, "I will never keep them in my house. What are you thinking of?"

"Oh, *do* take them, auntie!" prayed Emma. "If nobody will have them, they must be killed."

"Tut, tut, children," said the dear old lady, by way of comforting. "They are only a couple of animals, after all."

"Animals?" ejaculated Emma. "It's Ada and her pup, Aunt Lizzie, please remember"

Upon this the four comrades went away in a rather disconsolate state of mind. After all, Aunt Lizzie was not as nice as they had thought her. Now she should not get the two sweet animals, even if she went down on her knees and prayed for them.

They went from one house to another. At every place they presented their Christmas gift, but without success. It was continually declined, and the situation grew more and more painful.

Now they were, as above described, rushing onward in high speed.

Suddenly Emma stopped, flushed and breathless "I cannot walk farther," declared she; "I am getting too tired. But let us go and make Uncle Peter a Christmas present of Ada and the pup!"

"No, I am afraid of that," answered John; "Uncle Peter is *so* queer, says mama; he can't bear to see any one around."

"**Yes**, but mama says that he has humane feelings, anyway. I don't know what *that* is. I heard
mama say that he had once had great sorrows.
Now, I don't know what that is, either; but some
days ago I gave him the first stocking I had made
for my big doll, and he smiled at it, and kissed me.
Let us go and bring him our Christmas presents!
I wonder what mama means by great sorrows, but
it must be something dreadful." Emma turned
around and led the procession, until all were standing in a row before Uncle Peter's rocking-chair.

"Here, Uncle Peter," say the children—"here we
bring you Ada and her pup; they are a Christmas
gift for you."

"How is that?" asks Uncle Peter, in wonder.
But Emma's arms are already around his neck, and
she sobs into his ear: "Ada and her pup were to
be killed, and that would be so—so dreadful to
us, such a great sorrow, Uncle Peter. You know
what that means, for you have had some yourself,
haven't you!"

What is the matter with Uncle Peter? He starts,
suddenly pushing Emma away from him, presses
both hands against his forehead, but suddenly jumps
from his chair and walks up to Ada, addressing her
in his deep, strong voice: "Do you wish to stay by
such an old fellow as I, old lady?"

Ada proceeds to make an appropriate remark in
her own tongue. Uncle Peter seems to understand
her answer; he turns to the children, exclaiming:

"I never heard the like! Ada says she intends to keep Christmas here for her pup, and we are invited, all three!"

How *could* Ada think of such a thing! Well, there is no moment to be lost; it is already late in the afternoon. A number of hurried visits are made to many different stores, and at length the preparations are finished.

A beautiful Christmas-tree is lighted in Uncle Peter's study. His furniture locks quite amazed at the strange spectacle.

But the door is opened, admitting the surprised faces of mama and papa. Uncle Peter nods and beams upon them with his large, benevolent face.

"Children, children!" exclaims mama. "Why did you run away in such a manner? Papa and I were very uneasy about you."

"We could not come home yet, mama," objects John. "Ada keeps Christmas for her puppy, and we are all invited, you know!"

A ray from the Christmas star kisses his eager, upturned face, and his mother follows its example.

III

NUMBER 101

"Follow me," whispers the twinkling star, "to narrow dwellings, where hearts grow faint and weary; to dreary places, where the name which a mother gave her child is changed into a number."

There is a large and quiet-looking building, lonely, situated in the outskirts of the city, with high and firm walls, the monotony of which is broken by no ornament except the regular lines of small, curious windows. These look, in fact, rather like the small, deep-set eyes of an old, irascible bachelor than spaces through which the sunlight, which God gave to mankind before anything else was created, can penetrate the darkness within and conjure away the shadows.

Twilight settles upon the large building, and one window after another is lighted. They look like long rows of tired, sleepy eyes, as they shine forth, in a thoughtless, passive manner, through the misty evening air. Do they tell us of the many deadened hopes and stifled aspirations of those who dwell under the roof of this building?

They do. Behind every one of them a spoiled life is slowly dragged along under the benumbing influence of the sombre place, under a code of rules and regulations as rigidly enforced as observed, under a system which induces forgetfulness on one important point above all—namely, that man's acts are not always man's nature.

Prisoner Number 101—name forgotten—is proud of having behaved well. Soon his time will be out, so he will again become an honest member of society. The crime was bought by the sacrifice of so-and-so many years of freedom, bought and honestly paid for. An honest deal, and nothing else, says Number 101.

I see him behind the little window at the right end of the second row, as he sits on a narrow bench, leaning forward, with his elbows upon his knees and with folded hands, glancing through the iron bars into the darkness outside, towards one little twinkling star high above the black earth and its codes of rules and regulations.

Number 101 is thinking, although there is — officially — no personality behind the thoughts. "Halloo!" cry the thoughts, undaunted by the heavy doors and iron bars; but the well-known places and figures do not return the greeting as confidentially as of old. There is one sweet, girlish face at the remembrance of which the prisoner's heart waxes warm, although it is not known—officially—that Number 101 possesses a heart; but it turns away from him like all the other acquaintances, whereat he clinches both hands against the small speck of the dark sky visible through the little window in the wall.

"That is not the right way to treat a prisoner who served his time," say the thoughts. "Beware! Any one who scoffs at me, exonerated as I am now, will be duly punished, like all other offenders. There is justice even for an offender when he has paid his debts to justice."

The thoughts pursue their course from one place to another, and Number 101 holds his head high, for he has paid his debts.

But in the centre of the whirling mass of thoughts there is one dark point which seems to frighten the thinker, like a vacuum horrifies nature. It seems possessed of a singular influence, both attractive and repulsive. The thoughts are afraid of this dark point, and yet they must approach it. Prisoner Number 101 buries his head in his two strong hands, but "visions come again" of things departed.

A woman in a ragged dress is standing on the market-place. She has sold her last lamb; baby's lambkin must change owner, that money might be procured. Even baby cannot live on her love for her sweet lambkin; even sweet baby—healthy and fresh in her rags—needs a crumb of bread now and then.

The poor woman sells her lamb, and her five thin fingers are eagerly seizing an equally thin roll of paper money. Tears rise in her eyes, as they came into a pair of blossom - blue ones at home when lambkin departed.

There is a rush of feet. Five strong fingers grasp the tiny roll of money with which lambkin was bought, and Prisoner Number 101 darts away into the crowd.

"Stop thief!"

Number 101—name already forgotten—stands before the bar and tells frankly of his guilt.

"How could you do it?" asked the judge, looking from his strong, well-built figure to the poor woman in her ragged dress.

The strong man bends his head before the stern gaze of the man of law. He wishes to fall on his knees and pray forgiveness; but to produce a scene in the court-room where inquisitive eyes are watching from every corner, trying to catch every bit of sensational news—that would never do. So the guilty man hides his feelings, and no sensation occurs, and as there are no extenuating circumstances, he must pay his debt in full.

Number 101 lifts his head and waves his hand at the dark thoughts, repeating: "I have paid it all."

"You have not," say the thoughts.

"I have," firmly asserts the prisoner.

"You could not," repeat the thoughts. "Do you not know that you could pay none of your debts, even by sacrificing your whole life?"

"When I leave this room a free man, I am exonerated, and no one will dare say a word about the debt," continues the lonely man.

But the thoughts are persistent, and resume: "People will scowl at you, and close their doors on you; nay, even be afraid to touch you. No man or woman can ever blot out the brand for theft which you carry."

"They dare not do it. There is justice in the land, and I am exonerated. No one shall scowl at me."

Steps sound and resound in the spacious halls outside; at length a rap at the door starts Number 101 from his revery. At nine o'clock the light is made out; it is time to go to bed, and the prisoner knows it.

At nine sharp Number 101 is in bed, like all other prisoners. The light goes out, and darkness rolls its mask down over the lonely man. But thoughts will roam about, so far and wide, until one little figure after another finds its way in under the mask, and carry the sleeper's spirit away into dreamland.

No man or woman can ever blot out—

The little twinkling star lifts the dark veil, and sheds its silver rays upon the figure in the narrow bed, in the narrow room, behind the high walls.

Prisoner Number 101 has gone to sleep with a smile upon his face, dreaming that he has returned to baby, for whom he brings a new lambkin with beautiful, white wool, and a golden collar.

HERE was once a man who had three daughters, each of whom was married to a mountain troll. Their father once wished to pay them a visit, and before he went away his wife handed him a rather dry loaf of bread. When he had walked along for a while he became tired and hungry, so he seated himself on the eastern slope of a hill, and commenced eating his dry bread. The hill was suddenly opened, and his oldest daughter appeared before him, saying: "Why do you not come in and see me, father?" "Well," answered her father, "had I known that you were living here, and if I had seen any entrance, I should have walked in."

Soon afterwards the troll returned home. His wife told him that her father had come, and asked him to go and buy meat for a soup. "Oh, we may have that much more easily," said he, whereupon he ran a large iron nail into a heavy piece of timber and knocked his head against it, tearing large pieces of meat out of his cheeks. He seemed to suffer no inconvenience from this, and they all had a wholesome soup. Afterwards the troll gave the old man a sack filled with money, whereupon they separated, the man returning home. When he arrived not very far from his house, he suddenly remembered that one of his cows was sick, so he left the sack in the road, and, hurrying on, asked his wife if the cow had died.

"What are you thinking of!" exclaimed she; "no cow has died." "Well," answered he, "then you must come out and help me carry in a sack of money." "A sack of money!" repeated his wife, very much astonished. "Yes," replied he, "a sack of money, indeed. Is that so remarkable?" Although she did not trust his story, she obeyed, and followed him to the place. But when they arrived there no money was to be found. A thief, in the mean time, had carried it away. Now the wife became angry and grumbled at her husband. "Well, well," he said; "never mind the money! I learned something which I will not forget." "What did you learn?" inquired she. "Never mind!" repeated he. "I will not forget it."

Some time after, the man desired to visit his second oldest daughter. His wife again handed him a loaf of dry bread, and when he became hungry and thirsty he seated himself on the eastern side of a hill and commenced eating. While he was thus engaged his second oldest daughter came out of the hill and asked him to step in, which he did cheerfully enough. Soon afterwards the troll, her husband, returned home. It had become dark, so his wife asked him to go and buy some candles. "Candles!" he repeated, "those we have already." Upon this he thrust his fingers into the fire. When he drew them out they were themselves luminous, without being hurt, in any respect, by the flames. The old man was now given two sacks filled with money, and stumbled homeward. When he came near his house, he again remembered that his cow was yet sick; he therefore left the sacks in the middle of the road, ran on home, and asked his wife if the animal had recovered. "What is the matter with you?" said his wife. "Why do you come running as if the house were ready to fall? You need not trouble yourself a bit; the cow is well." He then asked her to assist him in carrying home the two sacks of money. Although she did not believe his tale, he pleaded and talked until she consented to follow him. But when they arrived at the place a thief had again been there, and the money was gone. No wonder that the wife abused her husband. He said, however, only these words: "Well, you don't know what I have learned!"

In a short time the man prepared himself to visit his youngest daughter. When he arrived at a hill, he sat down and ate some of the dry bread which his wife had given him. His daughter came forth immediately—this was the southern side of the hill— and took him into her dwelling. Soon her husband, the troll, made his appearance. As they needed fish, his wife wished him to go and buy some. He answered, however, that they might procure some much more easily : she must give him her winnowing-trough and her bale. Upon this the troll and his wife seated themselves in the trough and put to sea. When they had arrived at a short distance from the shore the troll asked : " Are my eyes green?" " No," answered his wife, " not yet." When they had proceeded a little farther he repeated his question. " Yes," answered she ; " now they are green." The troll immediately jumped into the water and baled so many fish out of the sea into the trough that soon it could hold no more. When they had landed, the whole company had a hearty meal. The troll finally gave his father-in-law three sacks filled with money, and with these he started home.

When he had almost reached his house, he thought once more of the cow. Placing the sacks of money on the ground, and his wooden shoes on top of them, to prevent their being stolen, he hastened to his house, asking if the cow were still alive. In the mean time, however, the same thief that had been there before had his eye upon the money. He stole it all, leaving the wooden shoes behind him. When the couple came out for the sacks and found nothing but this pair of old shoes, the wife scolded at a great rate. Her husband remained quiet, however, saying only : " Never mind the money ! I have learned a good lesson." " What did you learn ?" asked she ; " it would be well worth knowing." "Yes," replied he, "you will know some day !"

Some time afterwards the wife wished for some soup, and said to her husband: "Will you not go to town and buy a good piece of soup-meat?" "We don't need to buy it," answered he, "it may be had more easily;" whereupon he knocked his head against a large nail in the wall. The blood streamed from a wound in his forehead, and he was obliged to remain in bed for a long time thereafter. After he had finally recovered, one day it was found that there were no candles in the house, so his wife asked him to go and buy some. "No," said he, "that is unnecessary;" whereupon he thrust his hand into the fire. Of course he was severely burned and obliged to figure on the sick-list for another length of time.

When he was up again, it one day happened that they wished for some fish. Now the man deter-mined to show what he had learned; he asked for his wife's winnowing-trough and a bale, and they both put to sea. In a little while the man asked: "Are my eyes green?" "No," answered his wife, "how *could* they be green?" When they had gone a little farther he repeated his question. "What nonsense!" exclaimed she. "How could they *ever* become green?" "My dear wife," said he again, "will you not be good and say they are green?" "Why, yes; they are green," answered she.

As soon as the man heard this, out he jumped into the sea, with his bale, in order to bring up the fish.   He was obliged, however, to stay where he was, and was never seen again.

THE BULL AND THE PRINCESS AT THE
GLASS MOUNTAIN

N a certain town there once lived two families, each of which consisted of a man, his wife, and a grown son. When the one man's wife and the other wife's man died, the remaining couple was married, and thus the two boys came to live together. The man's son took care of the cows and a bull which was so large and savage that every one was afraid of him. The boy never had anything but dry bread-crusts to eat; but one day the bull asked him if he did not feel hungry. The boy told him he did. " Stroke my back, then," said the bull. The boy complied, receiving at once a butter-cake and a large piece of sausage which tasted splendidly. In the evening, when he returned home, he was unable to eat his supper, and his step-mother asked him, therefore, if the bull had not already given him some. This he denied, however.

The next day she sent her own son along to the pastures, and told him to watch and see if his step-brother received anything from the bull. It happened exactly as on the day before ; he stroked the bull's back, and received a delicious butter-cake and a large piece of sausage. He could eat no supper at night, and his step-mother at once declared that both the boy and the bull must be burned. There was now a large pile of wood heaped up, and the boy and the bull placed on top of it. But the boy at once seated himself on the animal's back, whereupon the bull rushed up to the woman, who was looking on, seized her on his horns, and threw her straight into th fire.

The bull now darted into the woods with the boy. In a little while they noticed some apple-trees bearing the most beautiful-looking apples. He was warned by the animal not to touch them, but the more he looked at them, the more he wished to eat one. The very moment he made this wish the forest begar to quiver, and the bull asked whether he had not broken the rules and taken an apple. He denied having done so. "Feel in your pockets," said the bull. There was, indeed, an apple in one of his pockets, but he was willing to throw it away. "That would not help us," said the bull again. At the same moment a troll with three heads came running towards them, roaring: "Why do you steal my apples?" "Come, if you dare !" cried the bull; and seizing the troll on his horns, he threw him high in the air. "You may have them all," shouted the troll, "if you will leave me alone." "That depends upon your giving us the black horse which is now in your stable," answered the bull. No, that would not do. So the bull again seized him, throwing him into the air as high as the tree-tops. "Yes, yes," yelled the troll; he was willing to give them what they wanted, if they would leave him alone. So they took the horse and departed.

When they came far into the forest, they saw some apples which were prettier even than the first ones, and the boy could not help wishing that one of them was his. He had hardly realized his wish before the forest commenced quivering, and a troll with six heads appeared before them. "Come here, if you dare!" cried the bull, seizing the troll and throwing him into the tree-tops. "Stop, stop!" called the troll. "Well," resumed the bull, "will you give us the spade and shovel which you have at home?" No, they could not have them. The bull again caught and pitched him from one tree-top into another. "Yes, yes," yelled the troll, "you may have them, if you will leave me alone." This they did.

After resuming their journey they reached in a little while some trees with apples more beautiful than those which they had already seen. "Now be sure and take none!" said the bull. The boy could not help wishing for some, however, and no sooner had his wish been realized than a troll with nine heads came forward. Like the two others, he was kicked about by the bull, until he promised to give them a bag of mist which he had in his possession.

They now proceeded on their journey until they arrived at two hills ; here they stopped, and the bull said to the boy: " Dig a hole in the ground and bury me here ; place the spade and the shovel on top of me, and cover me with earth. When you have done this, you must go to the palace yonder and apply for a position as groom. A year from to-day you must return and dig me up. Remember, however, to bring one dish of water, one of blood, and one of milk with you." He promised to remember and to obey, but of course he did not like to bury his friend. Having done so, nevertheless, he walked up to the palace, where he had no difficulty in securing a place as groom. Afterwards he was told that in a few days a troll was to come and carry the beautiful princess who lived there away with him. She would be placed on the top of a glass mountain, however, and if any one could ride up to her and take a silver apple from her hand on the first day, a golden apple on the second day, and kiss her on the third day, he would be allowed to marry her. Of course there was a great stir and doings around the palace, when, on the appointed day, a large number of men tried to ascend the mountain. No one was able to reach the top, and several even broke their arms and legs in attempting. Finally the boy came riding on his black horse. He was dressed in black, and rode straight up to the princess, from whose hand he took the apple. She, too, was dressed all in black.

The next day the same thing was repeated. No one but the young man reached the top of the mountain. He was dressed, like the princess, in yellow, and having reached her, he seized the golden apple from her hand.

On the third day the boy appeared in a white dress. He rode up to the princess, who was herself dressed in white. But when he bent down and kissed her, she managed to tear a small piece of cloth from his coat, and put it aside. All the spectators were, of course, very anxious to know the name of the clever person who had been able to ride where a great many skilled and practised noblemen had broken their limbs. Hence, they surrounded the mountain from all sides to meet him when he came back; but when he perceived this, he opened the bag of mist which he had carried along with him, emptied it at the top of the mountain, and thus produced such a fog that no one saw him when he passed, in spite of their careful watch.

As they were very anxious to know who had saved the princess, the king issued invitations for a great party to all who had taken part in the chivalrous sport. He intended to find out if the man whom all desired to see were among them. The jewellers now became very busy. Every one who could afford it had silver and gold apples made, but none of them was found to be the right one. Finally the groom came forward on his black horse. Riding up to the princess, he threw his silver apple in her lap, and she recognized it at once as her own; but the young man immediately rode away again.

The next day all the guests were required to produce their golden apples. Many came and showed their treasures, but the right one was not found. At last the groom came riding along, dressed in yellow, and flung his apple into the lap of the princess, who knew it again as her own. He rode away at once, however, before any one had seen him.

On the third day the king ordered that if the stranger should appear, the gates must be closed as soon as he entered the palace, in order that it might be known who he was. The young man appeared in due time, mounted on his horse and dressed in white, and the gates were promptly closed as soon as he had entered the court-yard. It did not seem to affect him in the least; he rode forward, apparently unconcerned. Of course every one recognized him as the one who had ascended the glass mountain, and they perceived that a corner of his coat was missing. Now all became very busy in tearing off bits of their coats, but to no effect at all; for when they were all brought into the presence of the princess, the piece of cloth in her possession fitted exactly, and only, to the groom's coat, and she was at once sure that he, and no one else, had saved her, and wished to be married to him. At first the king was not quite satisfied, hearing that the young man was only his groom; but as the princess insisted, and as the boy was also willing to be married to her, it was determined that the wedding should take place at once. Now the boy asked permission to drive out for a few hours; when he returned he would be ready for the ceremonies. This was granted, a carriage made ready for him, and as the princess desired to join him, they drove away together. She thought it singular that he took milk, and blood, and water with him, but said nothing.

Of course he intended to go to the place where he had buried the bull, for this was the day exactly a year ago when he had consigned him to the grave. At the time that the carriage arrived in the neighborhood of the two hills, he bid the coachman stop, and alighted, carrying his articles with him. The princess asked permission to follow, but this he refused.

He soon found the place. When some of the earth had been removed, the spade and the shovel did the rest of the work, and before long the bull stood before him, saying: "Cut off my head, place it at my tail, and wash it in the blood, the milk, and the water." As soon as this was done, a beautiful prince stood there in place of the animal. He told the boy how the queen, his step-mother, had converted him into a bull. The king, his father, thought him dead long ago.

The prince then seated himself on the horse which had come running after them, and they went together to the princess who was waiting in the carriage. When she recognized her long-lost brother, she expressed unbounded joy over his return. All three returned to the palace, where a great sorrow had in the mean time prevailed, on account of the sudden death of the queen. When, however, the rescued prince told how she had treated him, and how it was decreed that she must die the moment he was set free, there were no grounds for distress, and the king declared it served her right. The marriage was now celebrated with much pomp and splendor. Afterwards the king felt sorry that the prince, his son, was unable to inherit the throne after him. "However," he said, "you may marry the princess in the country next to mine." "So I will," declared the prince, and accordingly he went over to another country, married the princess, and inherited *her* father's throne, and there they lived agreeably and well contented.

NCE there was a little girl who had an old grandmother—such a very, very old grandma, with white hair, and wrinkles all over her face. But Katherine, the little girl, loved her, and did all she could to please the old lady.

Katherine's father owned a very large house, the front of which turned towards the south, receiving all the splendor of the bright sunshine. But the old grandmother occupied a room at the north side, where no sunshine would come. Kate often wondered why it never took a notion to peep into her grandmother's room, and one day she asked her father why it was so.

"The sunshine cannot reach her room," answered her father, "because it is at the shady side of the house."

"Why can't we turn the house around, papa, and have grandma's room placed where the light may reach it?" inquired the little girl.

"You little goose," replied he, "do you think we can turn the whole house so easily? But even if we could, why, we should live ourselves in the shade!"

Katherine was, however, not yet satisfied, but continued: "Will grandma never have sunshine in her room, then?"

"No," returned her father, smilingly, "of course not—that is, unless you can carry it over to her."

After that day Kate often wondered how she could manage to bring the sunshine over to her grandmother's room. She looked at the flowers in the open air. They seemed to support the bright rays that rested like a golden net upon every object in the quivering summer air· even the green foliage and the glittering wings of the birds seemed to support their floating splendor. When Kate herself walked out and in she often thought that the shining mass clung to her face and her clothes. Could she not keep it with her, then, and bring it into the little, dreary room at the shady side of the house? She resolved to try.

Every bright day she went out and in the garden, where the sun would shine on her, and hastened back into the old lady's room. As soon as she had crossed the door-step, the rays were, however, gone—at least, she saw them no more. Still, her grandmother said: "I am always glad to see you come in, my little girl; it is dark and dreary here, but as soon as you open the door the bright sunshine peeps out of your eyes and cheers the room about me."

THE SUNSHINE

Katherine wondered much at her grandmother's words, and tried to find out, by looking in the mirror, whether the sunshine really did peep out of her eyes. She saw none; but one day after another she brought the beautiful sunshine to the old lady, who told her stories about kings and heroes until the little girl's eyes sparkled with joy.

When Kate became grown, she often thought of those happy days. She lived long enough to feel how necessary it is that childish eyes and smiles should bring sunshine into dark and dreary places, and how often our old friends need to feel the presence of a bright little ray amidst their sorrows and troubles.

For life is not all gladness and pleasure. Thank God, most of it is; but every bright day grows from a dark night!

HERE was once a man who had a cow which he decided to sell. He went to six different butchers, secured bargains with them, and received ten dollars in advance from each one of them, telling them to come to his house at any time and take the animal away.

In due time the first butcher came to his house and received the cow. When the rest came and found the barn empty, they became angry and had him summoned to appear in court.

The man went about every day trying to think of some manner in which he could settle this difficult affair, but without being able to find a way out of his troubles. At length he became quite desperate, and in this state of mind appeared in town on the day appointed. When he walked through the streets, looking considerably perplexed, he was hailed by a lawyer who happened to see him from his window, and who observed that he was much oppressed. "What ails you, my friend?" inquired the lawyer, running into the street and catching

"'OH, PSH A-AW!'"

the man by his arm. "It will be of little use for me to tell you," answered he, "because I need a friend who can both turn and twist things around." "Why," exclaimed the lawyer, "that is my very occupation!" Whereupon he seized the man firmly by the collar and pulled him into the house. Now the sinner made a confession before him, telling him how it had all happened. Could the lawyer help him out of this difficulty? "Yes," was the answer, "and very easily, too: When you are brought into the court-room, and the questioning begins, you must answer only 'Oh, pshaw!' Whatever they say to you, you must make no other reply."

When the man was brought before the judge, and the question was put to him whether he had sold the cow, as reported, he answered: "Oh, pshaw!" The judge looked at him over his glasses, and repeated: "I ask you whether you sold your cow to these six men and received in advance ten dollars from each of them?" "Oh, pshaw!" said the man again. Now the judge became excited; however, he stepped forward and shouted into his ear: "Did you sell your cow to these six men?" The man, on his part, bent forward, yelling into the judge's ear, "Oh, psh — a — aw!" As he looked quite sincere, and no other reply could be had from him, the judge turned to the six men, saying: "There is no way in which you can be righted, my friends. This man is insane, and all that we can do is to let him go. You may go," concluded he. "Oh, pshaw!" promptly was the reply. So the policemen grasped him by the collar and kicked him out of the court-room.

The lawyer watched the street from his window, and as soon as he saw his friend trudging along he called him in. The man stopped and gazed at him. "Come in!" called the lawyer. "I must now be paid for the good advice I gave you."

"Oh, pshaw!" answered the man, trudging homeward.

N a country far, far away there once lived a great and powerful king who had three sons, all of whom he loved as dearly as a father can love his children. The two older ones were very handsome and intelligent, while the youngest was of little account. Peter was his name, and, as a rule, his brothers and comrades made a fool of him whenever they saw their chance; they called him Peter Humbug. The king, however, liked them all equally well, and when he reached old age he did not know how to avoid wronging two of them by electing one as his successor to the throne.

In those days it was a custom with the kings to extend a heavy iron chain all around the palace in order to prevent the common people from running into the court-yard. The chain which was now serving that purpose had become so well worn, however, by rust and wear, that the king thought seriously of having a new one made. As he was a wise man, who always knew how to manage his affairs easily and suitably, he thought that here was an opportunity to kill two birds with one stone—namely, at one time to decide who would be his successor, and to secure a new chain for the palace. Therefore, he said to the princes : "Now you must all three set out for the purpose of getting a new chain for the palace. A year from to-day you shall return, and he who brings the longest chain will be my successor to the throne after my death."

The two oldest boys at once departed. The one secured work with the ablest blacksmith he could find, while the other, who considered himself much more clever than his brother, was engaged by a coppersmith, thinking that copper could be worked more easily than iron.

Peter Humbug was for some time uncertain whether he wished to depart or not; he thought that his brothers were more able and skilled than he. But when the king told him to do his best he trudged away. Of course he had no idea what to do, or how to make such a chain as his father wished ; so he walked straight into the country, until he entered a large forest where, at length, he lost his way. Evening and night found him walking about among the trees. At length he discovered a light shining in the distance, and when he followed the direction towards it he finally reached a small hut. Having knocked at the door, he heard some one call "Come in !" whereupon he opened it and crossed the threshold. Imagine his surprise when he found no one within except a big white cat seated comfortably in a chair. Supposing that no one but the cat could have responded to his knock, he turned to her, inquiring if he could secure a resting-place in the house. The cat told him that he was welcome. "But," she added, "since you come so late, you are no doubt hungry." Peter Humbug replied that there was some truth in that, and the cat now proceeded to tell him where to find what he needed to eat, whereupon Peter did justice to the viands. When the meal was finished, the cat pointed to a bed, telling him that he might go to sleep whenever he desired. Tired as he was, he soon slept soundly.

Next morning the cat expressed her wish to know who he was and where he was going. Peter told all, adding that he had, beforehand, given up the hope of securing such a long chain ; in fact, he knew not where to find or how to procure it. "If you will serve me," said the cat, "you shall have nothing to do but wash and comb me three times every day. Of course you will receive no wages, and the meals will be exactly like the one which you had last night." "That might be well enough, after all," answered Peter ; "time will pass, then, until the year comes around." He stayed with the white cat, washed and combed her three times a day, and passed the rest of his time in the woods. When the year had passed, the cat said : "Now you must return home, Peter ; both of your brothers will do the same." But Peter did not care to do so, since he could carry no chain with him. "You must do it, anyway," said the cat, "and I promise to give you a chain which is better than those of both of your brothers. Carry home the chest which you see standing in the hall, and when your brothers have showed their chains, you must open this chest, which contains a chain longer and better in every respect than all others." Peter thanked the cat, bid her good-bye, took the chest, and left the little house in the forest.

When he reached home, his brothers had already arrived. The king proceeded to ask the oldest to produce his chain. The young man opened a strong coffer and pulled out a heavy iron chain, which he tried in the place reserved for it. It held the exact measure, and was in every respect satisfactory. Then the second oldest came with his masterpiece, a copper chain, which reached twice around the palace. "Now, Peter," said the king, addressing his youngest son, "let us see what you have brought." Opening his chest, the boy drew out a very heavy chain made of pure gold, which held three times the right measure. Every one agreed with the king that Peter had done best of all, because his chain was not only the longest, but also a costly treasure.

The two older brothers were by no means content with the result of the contest. They had been sure of winning the prize, and considered Peter Humbug a poor fellow to manage a kingdom.

So at length they contrived to induce the king to send them away once more, this time for the purpose of getting money: He who returned with the largest amount of money was to inherit the kingdom. The king assented, and the brothers departed, Peter Humbug the last, like the year before.

The two older brothers considered themselves sure of winning this time, for it takes a clever man to earn much money, and Peter could not at all boast of being clever. The oldest brother became a merchant and gained one hundred per cent. on all that he sold. The other established himself as a money-lender, extorting money from unfortunate people in a sinful manner.

Peter was not sure of what he wished to do. As he went along in deep thought he chanced to find once more the little house in the forest, where he was again received by the white cat. He stayed there all night, and next morning the cat asked him whether he was willing to stay another year on the same conditions as before. He assented, and during the whole year he washed and combed the cat three times a day, passing the remainder of his time among the trees. Time passed rapidly, and before Peter knew, the year had passed. "Now you must return home, Peter," said the cat one day; "your brothers have gone back already." Peter objected, as he had no money. "Take with you the chest which you will find in the hall," said the cat; "it contains money enough."

When Peter arrived, his brothers were there already, and the king now asked them to show how much they had managed to gain.

The oldest son had been clever enough to gather his money in copper coin, thinking that he would have most, both in regard to weight and to number. He had so much that he covered nearly one-half of the floor in the largest room with his money.

The second oldest son came next. He had silver coin enough to cover the remaining part of the floor.

Finally, Peter came in. "Well, Peter Humbug," cried they, "can you bid higher?"

Peter thought he could not, and he who had the silver money began already to rejoice. Soon, however, Peter had opened his chest and emptied its contents upon the floor. He spread it over the copper and the silver, and when he had finished this work —behold! no copper or silver piece was visible, but the whole floor glittered and sparkled with Peter Humbug's gold.

"Peter is the victor this time as well," declared the king, "and now it is certain that he will inherit the throne."

Peter's two brothers were not pleased to hear this; they objected that he was not competent enough for this responsible position, and finally they proposed that their father should allow them to seek a wife: He who returned within one year with the prettiest wife should be successor to the throne. Although the king was not altogether pleased with this proposition, mainly for Peter's sake, he assented, especially as Peter himself made no objection.

The two brothers thought that this time it was quite impossible for Peter to win. What princess in the world would care to marry a person like Peter Humbug?

Peter trudged along; but where should he go and find a pretty wife? He speculated and speculated, hardly knowing whither he was going, until he found himself again at the hut in the forest. Having knocked at the door and heard the cat call "Come in!" he ate and slept; and next morning the animal asked him why he had returned again. Peter told her that he was seeking a wife, but did not know how to find one. When the cat heard the circumstances, she said that he had better stay where he was. Peter did not know whether it would be of any use to him, as he had never seen a single human being around this place, and he must, of course, seek a beautiful princess, or some person of high rank and great beauty; but as the cat had helped him so well the two previous times, he followed her advice, however, and consented to stay on the same conditions as before.

One day passed like the other. When the cat was washed and combed, Peter was at liberty to roam about in the woods to his heart's content.

Time flew so rapidly that he was taken by surprise when one day the cat told him that a year had passed, and that he must return home, as both of his brothers were already there, each with his bride. Peter thought there was time enough, as he had not yet found a bride for himself. "You have served me faithfully for three years," said the cat, "and, therefore, I am determined to help you this time also. You must promise, however, to do exactly as I tell you." Yes, Peter was ready to do whatever she wished! "Take your knife," pursued the cat, "and cut my head off. As soon as you have done this, strip off my skin."

Peter said he could not do this, as she had always treated him so kindly. "You must do it, nevertheless," returned the cat, "if you wish matters to end well."

Thus Peter was obliged to obey. But as soon as he had cut off her head and began to skin her, a beautiful princess stood before him with a crown on her hair. She told him how an evil power had doomed her to remain in the shape of a cat until a prince declared himself willing to serve her for three years. "And," added she, "as you have done so, I am freed from the witchcraft, and ready to return home with you."

Peter was, of course, both surprised and pleased to see the beautiful princess appear before him; but he was much more delighted to learn that she was willing to become his wife. Now he must surely win the contest, for a prettier princess he had never seen in all his life.

"Let us enter the golden carriage which is waiting in front of the house," said the princess; "during our journey I will tell you more about myself." They entered the vehicle, and while Peter drove the horses, brandishing the whip over the animals to his heart's content, in boundless joy, the princess related her history: "My father was once a great and mighty king, and he lived happily with my mother, until she fell sick and died; whereupon my father married a queen who was a widow with one daughter. But this step-mother of mine was a witch, and when she realized that I was prettier than her own daughter, she was afraid that I might stand in her way. Therefore, she converted me into the shape of a white cat, and forced me to live alone in this large forest, until you came and released me. And so I have a twofold reason for liking you!" Peter looked at the young princess, and as she smiled sweetly at him, he stopped the horses in the middle of the forest to kiss her.

They soon reached the palace. On the front steps the old king and his two older sons, with their wives, were standing, anxious to know who could afford to drive in such luxury. When the carriage stopped below the steps they recognized Peter. He jumped from his seat, helping the princess to alight, and as soon as they had glanced at her they all admitted that she was the most beautiful. The two other princesses were very pretty girls, but their beauty did by no means reach that of Peter Humbug's fair and graceful bride.

It was thus decided that Peter should inherit the throne. He did so, in fact, shortly afterwards, when the old king had died, and his marriage with the princess had been celebrated with great splendor. Evidently he was a much better man than people expected him to be, for he ruled his land wisely and well. He was much beloved by his people. But the two older brothers went away to other countries, and no one ever knew what became of them.

NE day a man came along the road pushing in front of him a wheelbarrow containing a bushel of rye, which he intended to bring to the mill. He met another man, with whom he fell to talking.

"Good-morning, my friend! Is the road good?"

"I did not taste it."

"Was the mill agoing?"

"I did not meet her."

"Why!" cried the first, "you are a funny fellow, aren't you?"

"I am no fellow, for I am a married man, and so I was for the last twenty years."

"Good enough for you!"

"No, it was not so very good."

"Why not?"

"Because my wife was too old."

"Too bad, wasn't it?"

"No, it might ha' been much worse."

"How so?"

"Because she had a house and **a heap of money.**"

"Pretty good for you, then!"

"No, it might have been better, for there was too much small coin in it."

"Bad enough for you!"

"No, it might ha' been worse, for we had enough to buy four good-sized pigs."

"Good for you!"

"No, it was bad enough, for when my wife melted off the lard, she set the house afire."

"That was pretty bad!"

"Worse it might ha' been, for I built a new one."

"That was good!"

"Not for me. When my wife went into the new house to see what it looked like, she fell down the stairs and broke her neck."

"Too bad! Too bad!"

"I don't say so, for I married again. My second wife is young and pretty."

"Good for you, then!"

"No, no. It might have been better, for she scolds and kicks me with a broomstick all the day long."

"That is too bad!"

"Yes, that *is* bad enough. Good-morning!"

HERE was once a king whose only daughter was so extremely conceited, and so much inclined to sneer, and in spite of her beauty and brightness so impertinent towards every one, that all the suitors who came to woo her turned aside in time and returned home again.

The king at length grew tired of this state of affairs. Hardly any of her equals desired to have anything to do with her, and her father finally swore that she would be forced to marry the man, whoever he was, who could silence her. " Let them try," said the princess; " let them try all they wish ; but if they fail they'll be hanged." " Very well," answered the king. So a decree was issued and posted at the street corners, and announced throughout the land.

There were many young men ready to make the trial, who thought they knew how to amuse one with fair words. They hoped to make their fortunes on this occasion. But they reckoned without their host, for when they were brought face to face with the princess, they invariably stopped short; which the princess never did. One after another was seized and hanged without mercy.

The king was quite vexed by watching how matters went. "You ruin all my young men," said he to his daughter; "the prospects for enlistments in our army are extremely bad." But he was, of course, obliged to act according to his own decree, as kings must always do.

Somewhere in the country there lived a farmer who had three sons. Their names were John, James, and Peter. The two older ones were said to be quite ready talkers; they "had graduated" from a high-school, and every one considered them capable of talking a leg off an iron pot. Indeed, they thought themselves great fellows, and neither of them for a moment doubted his ability to win the princess by means of his ready tongue, and to become king of the land. It was agreed between them that the one who should ascend the throne would make the other his prime-minister.

Their father was proud of them and believed in their superior oratorical powers; he therefore equipped them with fine clothes and beautiful horses with silver bridles, and thus they were ready to depart. "I wish to go along," said Peter, their brother. Hitherto he had been looked upon as a scapegoat, and his parents considered him a mere simpleton. He had been doing all the disagreeable work that no one else wished to do, such as turf-digging and the spreading of manure ; he slept among the ashes in the chimney-corner, and was generally called Peter Fiddle-de-dee. "I want to go, too," said he. "No," answered his brothers ; he must stay where he was, in his chimney-corner—that would suit him best. "I am pretty enough," continued Peter. "I ask for no new clothes." All that he wanted was a horse to ride on ; whether it was good or bad, young or old, would not matter. He was only laughed at, however ; his father was unwilling to grant him permission to ride even the oldest mare in the stable, and said that if he desired to go he must be contented with his own legs. "It is all the same," cried Peter, "for I will try to make my fortune," and so he trudged along after his two stately brothers.

When they had travelled a short distance Peter made a jump, and exclaimed : "Look what I have found !" "What did you find ?" inquired one of his brothers, turning around. It was only a dead crow which was lying in the road. "I must take it along to the palace," said Peter again ; "no one knows what use one may have of it." "Oh, you are a real fool !" said his brothers, spurring on their horses and fetching him a rap with their horsewhips. "Wait and take me along !" shouted he. "You may follow us as well as you can," answered they. Peter stuffed the dead bird into his pocket and quickened his walk.

In a little while he cried again : "Look what I have found !" His brothers did not even care to turn around and look ; but it was an old shoestring. "No one knows what it may be good for," said Peter, stuffing it into his pocket, and pursuing his way.

Soon he stopped again, shouting : "Look what I have found !" It was an old cork. His brothers were, by this time, far ahead. The cork, however, was passed down to the crow and the shoestring.

A few steps farther on he stopped again ; this time for the purpose of picking up a ram's horn. It went promptly into his pocket. When, the next minute, he found a similar one, it followed the other. "They may be of use, somehow or other," said he again.

When he had gone a little farther he again stopped ; this time before a large mud-hole. "Oh," cried he, "look at this, will you !" But no one heard him. "That may be of use," continued Peter, thrusting a handful of mud into his pocket ; "no one knows."

John and James had, in the mean time, reached the king's palace, where they announced their errand. "You know, I suppose, what you stake," said the guardsman to them. Yes, they knew all, they said, and so John was conducted into the room where the princess met her suitors. She was sitting in a gilded chair, on an elevated place, surrounded by all her court ladies. A short distance from her the king himself was sitting on his throne, and around him stood all his courtiers and counsellors.

"'LOOK WHAT I HAVE FOUND!'"

"How does your Royal Highness do?" inquired John, bowing politely to the princess. "I give you the deuce," answered she. "How in the world does that concern you?" Poor John stood aghast at this answer. So surprised and shocked was he, that he did not know what to say. Of course he was done with at once, and taken through a side door to be hanged.

Now James entered the hall. He could not guess what had become of John in such a hurry, but stepped briskly forward, and, bowing to the princess, he said: "How is your Highness?" "Highness!" exclaimed the princess; "we will give you highness before very long, my good fellow!" James was absolutely dumfounded. "Don't forget what you wish to say," continued the princess, sneeringly. James could not, in fact, utter a single word, and so he was brought out and hanged.

"Are there more suitors?" inquired the princess. Yes; the door was opened, and in came Peter Fiddle-de-dee, dusty and exhausted. He had been walking all the way, and when he arrived at the palace the guard showed him all the gallows. He lost no time in looking at them, but asked to be conducted to the princess.

"How do you do, Miss Fickle?" said Peter. "How hot it is here!" "It is not warmer to-day than it was yesterday," answered the princess. "I wonder what you are using all that heat for," pursued he; "why, it is warm enough here for roasting a pig."

"Yes," replied the princess, "yesterday we roasted eighteen of them ; to-day we had only two here." "That is well," said Peter, readily, "for then I have a chance to roast this crow ;" and up came the dead crow which he had found in the road. "It will split in the oven," observed the princess. "Here is a string which we will tie around it," answered Peter, producing the shoestring. "The grease will run out of its bill," continued the princess. "Then we may cork it up," returned he, showing her the cork. "You seem to keep your wits in your pockets," remarked the princess ; "but we will find a hook to hang you on !" "Hook?" repeated the boy, taking from his pocket one of the ram's horns ; "here is one, if you wish to have a look at it." "Well," exclaimed she, "I never saw the like !" "It is not far away," cried Peter, pulling forth the other ram's horn, and handing it to her. "Keep your muddy hands by yourself !" commanded the princess. "Oh no," returned Peter ; "if you wish to have some real fine mud, here it is." Now he brought forward the mud which he had found in the road, and threw it into the lap of the princess, soiling her beautiful white silk robe.

The princess was so enraged that she arose, swept the mud from her dress, stamped on the floor with both her feet, and burst into tears from mere desperation.

"Now you are silenced," said Peter, "and now

you are mine." The king at once arose and gave his consent. She had found the right man for a husband.

Peter married her and received one-half of the kingdom. When the old king died he had it all.

THE COVETOUS MAN

HERE once lived a man who was so covet-
ous that all who knew him despised him
with all their heart, either openly or se-
cretly. He was one of those men who
would be glad to put their wives and children, or
their old shoes, or worn-out clothes, out on high in-
terest. When his wife died, and he needed some
one to attend his house, he decided to choose another wife. His desire was, above all, to find one who
would eat as little as possible—namely, one-fourth of
a pea each day. She could under no circumstances
have more, for things must be saved up and kept
in store.

At length he found a woman who promised to
marry him, declaring that one-fourth of a pea every
day would satisfy her hunger abundantly.

When about a month had passed, the man thought
it singular that she was looking as stout and well
as when she came. He wondered how she could
live on so little. We understand, of course, that
he was careful to reserve for himself all that he
wished.

Thinking the matter carefully over, he decided upon asking his groom if he suspected her of eating the contents of the pots and pans while she prepared the meals. The groom answered that of course it might be so ; no one knew. His master asked him, further, if he had any idea how she could manage to satisfy her hunger without being caught in the act. The groom replied that the best way to watch her was to take a seat on the scraper while she was busy with the dinner. This the man decided to do, and see if his suspicion should be confirmed.

The groom was, however, a double-tongued fellow ; he went straight to the man's wife and warned her against eating from the pots and pans, as her husband would be watching her from the scraper.

In the forenoon, the next day, the groom helped his master to creep into the chimney, where he seated himself on the scraper. But his wife ordered the servant-girls to heap a good deal of turf on the fire, so that he might be snug and warm in his lofty seat. Of course she affected not to know of his presence in the chimney. The fire became very bright and warm, and the man suffered fearfully from heat and smoke, without daring to sneeze or call any one. At length his faithful servant came back and helped him down. But he was obliged to keep in bed for the next fourteen days, so much had he suffered.

Some time afterwards he was struck by the idea

that his wife might eat one thing or another when she dealt with the different articles in the pantry. He again asked his groom how he might observe her, and the faithful servant advised him to hide in a feather-bed which was lying in the pantry. This feather-bed could be opened at one end, and when he had slipped through the hole, the latter could be sewed together—a small opening being left through which he could command a view. At the same time the groom told the wife all, and advised her to be careful. When she came into the pantry she called the servant-girls and bid them hang the feather-bed over a line in the yard and beat it thoroughly, in order to free it from dust and prevent the feathers from being spoiled. The girls obeyed, beating the feather-bed to their hearts' content; but the man who was inside writhed like a worm under the blows without daring to utter a sound. When at length he escaped from his narrow prison, he was so severely bruised that he was obliged to seek his bed and to stay there for over a fortnight. His wife seemed much afflicted by his sickness, and asked him what was the matter. He answered that he was sick. "You ought not to eat more than I am eating every day," said she, "and you would feel much better."

When he arose he was again vexed by her good and healthy looks, so he again asked his groom what was to be done. No doubt she drank something when she went into the cellar and drew the glass of beer and wine which he had with every meal; this, no doubt, was the reason why she was as stout as when she first arrived. But how could he watch her? The groom advised him to knock the bottom out of a hogshead and creep into 't; when the bottom had been replaced the man could watch his wife by peeping through the bung-hole. He then told the woman of this plan.

When the wife came into the cellar she went from one end to the other, soliloquizing: "That hogshead needs a good cleaning." She called the girls and bid them bring some hot water, and when they came they were ordered to clean and shake the hogshead well. The girls did their best, and when they had finished their work the man was so scalded and blistered that there was hardly any skin left on his body. He remained sick for over four weeks. While he was confined to his bed it happened that a couple of cows belonging to the groom's parents died, and as their owners were very good and honest people, the covetous man's wife gave them two fine cows from her husband's stable to show how thankful she was for his kindness to her.

When her husband arose and missed his two best cows he became so vexed as to declare that he would lie down and die. His wife sent for a coffin and had him placed in it, and now every one thought him dead and gone. But on the day of his burial, when his coffin was lowered into the grave, he became terribly frightened and shouted to be set free, prom ising that he would allow his wife to eat all that she wished, and would take care of the poor and think of something else than hoarding money. "What does he say?" inquired the minister, who was a little deaf. "He promises to become a better man," answered the mourning widow. "Then make haste, children, and set him free," cried the minister. So the man came forth, and now he smiled and nodded pleasantly at every one. He kept his word to the letter. All who knew him agreed that, although rich, he was a model of a man and a husband. He lived long and happily with his wife, and the groom had his wages increased.

DOCTOR AND DETECTIVE

HERE was once an old farmer who had a great deal of turf, which he sold to customers in town. One day, when he drove to town with a large wagon - load, he chanced to meet a doctor. This worthy man came walking along in a stately manner, with a long pipe in his mouth, a cane in his hand, and a doctor's hat on his head. Under his arm he had a thick doctor-book. He was wrapped in a long, loose mantle. The farmer tipped his hat reverently, whereupon the doctor addressed him and said that he would like to buy the turf. They talked back and forth for some time, and finally came to an agreement in regard to the price. The farmer was to have the long mantle, the pipe and the cane, the doctor's hat and the book, and the doctor was to receive the turf. The bargain was closed. The farmer secured the doctor's articles and the doctor the farmer's turf, and then each went his own way.

It was late before the farmer returned home to his wife. She asked him at once if he had made a good bargain. When he produced the entire doctor's equipment she was not at all pleased, but wept, and asked, plaintively, how they would now obtain their bread and butter, since he had received no money for the turf. Her husband did his best to comfort her, saying that in a little while they would have all that they needed, for now he had decided to take up a doctor's profession. He put on the mantle and the doctor's hat, and with the long pipe dangling from between his teeth he sat from morning to night reading diligently in the large doctor-book. He looked exactly like a real doctor; no one would notice the slightest difference; but, nevertheless, no one came to consult him. Thinking the reason might be that no one knew of him, he at length decided to place a sign above his door stating, "*Here lives the Greatest Doctor in the World*," as he was sure this would at once turn the general attention towards him. He began to paint these letters on an old board. But as he had a very faint idea of writing—in fact, this was the first time he had ever tried the art—he wrote instead, "*Here lives the Greatest Detective in the World.*"

A few days afterwards the king happened to pass the house of the "Greatest Detective." "What in all the world is written on that sign?" said he, despatching one of his servants over to examine it closely. The servant reported that the sign advertised the greatest detective in the world. "Well," said the king, "I shall remember him and employ his services some day."

DOCTOR AND DETECTIVE

Some time after it happened that a thief entered
the Royal stables and stole two of the king's best
horses. A thorough search was made throughout
the land, both for the thief and the horses, but
without success. At length some one reminded the
king of the Detective, whose house they had passed.
"Exactly so!" cried the king. "Now we shall find
both thief and horses." He at once bid one of his
men go and seek the wise man's advice in the difficult problem. The man rode back, found the house,
knocked at the door, and walked in. Here he saw
the Detective sitting in front of the table, reading
in the large doctor-book. He took off his hat, bowed politely, and presented the king's compliments.
"I have come," he said, "to ask—" "That is all
very well," interrupted the doctor; "I know it already." "Oh yes, of course you do," answered the
messenger. "Will you kindly direct me where to
go and find them?" "Ye-es," replied the wise man,
turning the leaves in the large book before him,
"I will tell you what to do. Wait a moment." Now he
took out a slip of paper which he had found among
the leaves in the book, folded it, and handed it to
the messenger, directing him to go to the drug-
store and have this prescription filled. "Take the
medicine promptly," he concluded; "then you will
find them!" He looked just as wise and important
as any doctor in the land, and waved his hand graciously at the messenger as a sign that the audience was at an end.

The messenger lost no time in having the prescription filled, and as soon as the medicine was in his hands he took a pull at the bottle, and rode along as rapidly as he could, anxious to return to the king and relate his interview with the extraordinary man who seemed to know all beforehand. He had not gone very far, however, before the medicine began to act : of a sudden he was seized with a terrible headache, and was obliged to seek refuge in a house near the road, where he was very kindly received. Thinking that a little rest would do him good, he lay down on a sofa in a room facing the yard. The headache became more and more severe, however, and the poor fellow cursed the wise man and his medicine with all his heart. But just as he complained of his evil fate, he heard the neighing of a horse in the stable across the yard. He arose quietly and approached the window, listening attentively, as the neighing seemed familiar to him. Now the horse neighed once more. His doubts vanished, and at the same moment his headache seemed to also completely vanish. Silently he opened the window, jumped into the yard, crept into the stable, and at once found the stolen horses, which he immediately untied. A few hours later he stood before the king, who did not know how to praise and reward the wisdom of the Great Detective before whom nothing was, of course, concealed. He lost no time in sending him two hundred dollars as a token of his high esteem and his gratitude. When the doctor received the money he said to his wife that a doctor's trade seemed to be a very easy one, and she answered that his bargain, which had seemed to her a foolish one, was, after all, quite satisfactory so far.

Some time passed, when one day a beautiful gold ring belonging to the princess was stolen. A diligent search was made, but it seemed to have vanished altogether, with the thief. At length the Great Detective was named to the king as the right man to be consulted in this difficult affair. His Majesty lost no time in sending a beautiful carriage and a messenger, with an invitation to the great man : Would he kindly assist in finding the gold ring which had been stolen ? "Yes, I know it all," said he to the messenger who stood before him, bowing politely, "and I am willing to come." So he entered the carriage in his complete doctor's equipment, followed by his wife, whereupon they drove to the Royal palace. The king himself stepped forward and opened the carriage door to the worthy couple, bowing and scraping and making himself agreeable. He invited them to partake of a dinner; the following day they would begin the search for the ring. The wise man assented to this, and they proceeded to the dinner-table, which was, of course, laid in a splendid and gorgeous manner. The doctor whispered to his wife that she must remember how many dishes they had. When all had been seated, the door was opened and in came the servant with the first dish. The wise man looked at his wife, nodded, and said, "This is the first one." He did not see—in fact, no one did—that the servant turned as pale as a sheet, but busied himself with doing justice to the excellent things before him.

The servant, however, was fearfully frightened, and before returning to the kitchen he stopped behind the chair of the Great Detective, plucking him by the sleeve in order to attract his attention, but without apparent result. The dismayed man had nothing to do but return to the kitchen. He was one of the thieves, and, with two other servants, had stolen the ring and buried it in the Royal gardens under a large apple-tree. Pale and trembling from fear, he told his two friends how the Great Detective had said to his wife, "This is the first one"—meaning, of course, the first thief. As the second servant was to carry in the next dish, his two comrades told him to do his best and ask the wise man to step into the kitchen. Perhaps he could be induced to spare their lives.

As the servant entered the dining-hall, the doctor said to his wife, "This is the second one." She nodded. The servant grew white from fear and pulled him from behind by the sleeve. The great man thought, however, of nothing but the dishes, and did not feel the servant's endeavor to attract his attention. Thus the poor fellow was obliged to return to the kitchen without having accomplished his errand.

When the third servant entered the doctor said to his wife, "This is the third one." The servant pulled him, however, so violently by the sleeve that he turned in his chair, asking what he wanted. "Would he," whispered the unfortunate man, "go with him into the kitchen?" So he arose and followed him.

When he entered the kitchen the three servants implored him to spare them. He was right ; they had stolen the ring. The wise man looked keenly at the three culprits, bit his lips, and said that of course he had known it all the time. They were great rascals who deserved a severe punishment. He did not know whether he could really save them from the gallows. They now fell upon their knees and implored him to show mercy. They would be willing to give back the ring and pay him two hundred dollars if he would agree to keep their secret. This he promised, and before leaving them he told them to put the ring into a cake and serve it to the king's dog the next morning. They promised to do as he bid them.

Next morning the king began to speak of the lost ring. The Great Detective assumed his most important air, looked around him, and finally fixed his glance upon the big dog which was walking about on the floor. They were just eating breakfast, and when one of the servants carried around the dishes he stole a glance at the doctor and nodded, thus assuring him that the dog had eaten the cake. "Can you tell me where to find the thief and the ring?" pursued the king. "Both are in this room!" answered he. The king looked around in great astonishment. "Both in this room?" repeated he. "There is the thief," continued the doctor, pointing to the dog. Now the king was thoroughly amazed, and even angry; he thought the wise man made fun of him. "Kill the thief," said the doctor, sternly, "and you will be sure to find the ring." They did so at once, and, indeed, found the ring in the stomach of the animal.

The wise man received a great sum of money from the king, and afterwards the three servants paid him the two hundred dollars which they had promised him for keeping their secret.

But from this day the doctor became so famous that no one dared to steal. His very name frightened the thieves and made them control their evil instincts. Although he was no more called upon to detect stolen goods, he had already earned money enough for the rest of his lifetime. He lived happily many years, honored by every one in the land.

NCE there were a man and his wife who owned a very small farm; they had three sons. The oldest was called Peter, the second Paul, and the third Hans, who was considered somewhat feeble-minded, and was, therefore, generally called Hans Humdrum. As the boys grew up it became more and more difficult for their parents to provide for them, and when they were grown and too large to run errands for the neighbors, they were obliged to go farther away and take such service as they might find. Peter, the oldest, went away first. He received a shirt, a pair of stockings, and a large parcel of bread-and-butter; and having bid his parents good-bye, he started on his journey.

When he had walked a couple of miles he met a man who was driving along in great style, and who stopped, inquiring where Peter was going. The boy replied that he was seeking a place where he might secure work. "I have just left home to find some one to serve me," answered the man; "would you care to take the place?" "How much wages will you pay?" inquired Peter. The wages were a bushel of dollars for six months' service. "Before engaging you," pursued the man, "I wish to have a clear agreement. When the cock crows in the morning you must go to work and do all that I say. I like to keep my servants as long as possible, but from the beginning I engage them only for six months, and by the time the cuckoo begins to tune his voice our agreement is over. Then there is one more thing : I am disposed, myself, to be glad and contented, and do not like to have sour faces around me ; therefore I agree with my hired men that he who first becomes angry shall have a sound thrashing. If I become angry first, I at once give the man his wages, and he may go ; but if *he* shows ill-temper first, I give him his whipping and then throw him out of the door."

Peter considered this a singular agreement, so he thought it over before entering upon it. The man was not at all good looking. His mouth reached as far as his ears on both sides, and never had Peter seen a nose of such size and length. But as he smiled pleasantly and blinked so joyfully with his small, half-closed eyes, the boy thought that he was, perhaps, only playing a joke on him ; besides, the wages were extraordinarily high. He closed the agreement and at once entered upon his duties. Climbing into the carriage, he drove along with the man until they reached the farm where his future master lived. As it was towards evening when they arrived, Peter at once went to bed and slept soundly.

At six o'clock next morning the cock began to crow. Peter was dressed and at work in the barn before long threshing wheat, according to directions given by his Master on the previous night. He worked an hour, and still another, but no one called him to the breakfast-table. At length he laid down his flail and walked across the yard into his Master's dwelling-room. The man was sitting at the end of the table, but no breakfast was to be seen anywhere. Peter's mistress was, if possible, still more ugly than her husband; she was cross-eyed, and two long teeth reached far out of her mouth. A great many small, dirty children were crawling about everywhere; they fought one another, and yelled at the top of their voices. It looked as if they had already had their breakfast, but there seemed to be none for him.

"Are you hungry, Peter?" asked the farmer, winking and blinking and twinkling at him with his small eyes, until they almost seemed to disappear within the lids. "Yes," answered Peter, "of course I am hungry! I had no supper last night and no breakfast this morning, and I may well need it, as I have been threshing for over two hours." "Look at the writing above the door, Peter," continued the troll (for he was, of course, a troll, and no real farmer); "look above the door and see what is written there!" Peter looked, and read the following words:

"No breakfast until to-morrow." As he looked sorely disappointed, the troll continued: "Are you angry, Peter?" "No, certainly not," answered he, skulking away, quite abashed. Fortunately he had kept a piece of bread-and-butter; it now served him for breakfast, while he said to himself: "For one day such a freak matters little. Of course Master wishes to put me to a test, and to-morrow I can eat twice as much!" He threshed on until nightfall, when he went to bed with a hungry stomach.

Next morning the cock crowed at four o'clock. "The sooner we will have our breakfast," thought Peter, hurrying into his clothes and hastening to his work in the barn. Soon the flail began to move, but every little while he stopped and listened if any one called him for breakfast. Every second minute he opened the door and looked out, expecting to see some one appear and call him in. But no one came. At six o'clock he put his flail aside and went over to the house. Everything looked as on the previous evening. Of breakfast he saw nothing at all, and his Master was sitting at the end of the table looking pleased and satiated, while his wife made a great noise with the many children, who did not seem to suffer from want of food.

"Are you hungry, Peter?" asked the farmer, grinning all over his ugly face. "I suppose I ought to be hungry by this time," answered the boy; "yesterday I had nothing to eat, and to-day I have been working two mortal hours. Yes, I ought to be hungry, indeed !"   "Look at the writing above the door, Peter," continued the farmer, smiling blandly at him.   Peter read the same words as on the day before : "No breakfast until to-morrow."   "Yes," he said, "this is to-morrow, and I am tired of such foolishness.   One cannot work without eating." "You are not angry, I suppose," resumed the farmer, just as kindly as before.   Yes—and Peter swore to it—he *was* angry, for that was not the right way to treat the servants.   "Well," said the troll, "no doubt you remember the agreement between us !" In less time than it can be told Peter received as sound a thrashing as he had ever dreamed of, and the next moment he found himself outside of the gate, sore all over his body, and hardly able to walk away.   It took him many days to return home, and he was obliged to stay in bed for quite a length of time.   His parents gave him no consolation, but told him that he had behaved himself in a wrong manner.   No doubt his Master had only wished to put him to a test ; a bushel of dollars was too good wages to throw away in such a careless manner.

Paul now set out to find the place.   He had a large package of bread-and-butter and his clothes in a bundle, and when he followed the road which Peter had pointed out for him he was fortunate enough to meet the farmer, who came driving along. He stopped and asked Paul where he was going, and when he learned that the boy was seeking a place, he offered him one.   The agreement was the same as in Peter's case. Paul worked hard for three days and received neither bite nor sip. Finally he lost his patience, received his thrashing, and returned home in a miserable state.

While the old folks doctored their two oldest sons, cursing the cruel Master, Hans Humdrum went around and said nothing. One morning he was gone, no one knew where. He knew it himself, however, for he followed the road described by Peter and Paul, and as luck would have it he happened to meet the old farmer with the long nose and the smiling face. When he stopped and inquired where Hans was going, he offered him a place on his farm. "How much wages will you pay?" inquired Hans. "I will give you a bushel of dollars for six months' service," answered the man, repeating the agreement which we already know. "We will get on pleasantly together," declared Hans. "I hope so," answered the troll, and laughed so heartily that Hans could see all his long teeth; "you will stay with me until the cuckoo tunes his voice; then our agreement is fulfilled, if we do not part earlier. Every morning when the cock crows you must arise, and you will have to do all that I tell you." Yes, Hans was willing enough to agree upon this, and so they drove on together. They reached the farm, and without receiving any supper Hans slept during the whole night in the room which his brothers had occupied before him.

At six o'clock next morning the cock crowed.

Hans arose and went to the barn, as he was told. When he had worked for an hour without being called to breakfast, he went into the house where the fine-looking troll family was assembled. The troll himself was sitting at the end of the table; his wife rested in the chimney-corner, and all the ugly children were romping about the room. "Good-morning," said Hans; "it is time for breakfast, is it not?" "Our agreement says nothing about that," replied the other; "but read what it says above the door." Hans was no ready reader, but at length he succeeded in spelling the words, "No breakfast until to-morrow." "To-morrow is far ahead," said Hans, "and we may think of that when the time comes." "You may look to the rye for your breakfast," remarked the troll, grinning at the boy, who was retreating through the door. Hans made no reply, but returned to his work threshing rye. Towards dinner-time he filled a sack with rye and carried it to an innkeeper who lived in the neighborhood, and to whom Hans said: "My Master and I have agreed that I shall receive no breakfast at the house; he has told me to look to the rye. Will you board me for this bushel of rye?" The innkeeper was willing to do this, and Hans received an excellent meal and provisions besides in his scrip. Upon this he returned to his work.

As it happened the first day, it did on the following days also. The letters above the door were always the same, but Hans was as complaisant and obedient as when he entered upon his duties. The troll asked him each morning, "You are not angry, Hans?" The boy promptly answered, "No, I have no reason to be angry."

On the fourth morning, when Hans came into the room and the farmer showed him the letters above the door, he turned around, intending to return to the barn, when the troll said: "Are you not angry, Hans?" "No," answered he, "not particularly." "Have you had nothing to eat for these three days?" continued the troll. "Yes," replied Hans; "I had all that I needed. I looked to the rye, as Master said. The innkeeper is willing enough to give me all that I need for a bushel of rye every day." "What do you say?" shouted the troll. "I hope Master is not angry with me," pursued Hans. "No, no, by no means," eagerly returned the troll; "but you had better leave the threshing and do something else. You had better plough some of the fields. Load the plough on a wagon and drive out. My dog will go in front of you; where he lies down you must begin ploughing, and when he returns home you must follow him back to the house." Hans obeyed; but towards noon he began to feel hungry. As the dog remained lying in the grass, and seemed to have no intentions of moving, the boy seized his whip and reached him a good blow across the back, which caused him to jump up and run homeward at great speed. Hans skipped

"THE ANIMAL JUMPED THE GARDEN FENCE"

down, cut the traces, jumped on the horse again, and rode after the dog at a furious rate. When they reached the house the animal jumped the garden fence, and Hans followed him promptly. Unfortunately one of the horses fell and broke his leg, however, and the other ran into one of the hedge-stakes. Thus both horses were disabled. The troll, who heard the uproar, came running out, but Hans said: "I acted upon your instructions, Master. I followed the dog, and here we are. You are not angry, I hope, because both of our horses were spoiled." "Nonsense!" replied the troll; "no, I am not angry. Come in and have some dinner." He really began to be afraid of the boy who obeyed him so literally.

Hans received both dinner and supper, and the next morning he was ordered to tend the swine. There were about fifty of them, and beautiful, fat animals they were. "Let them go wherever they wish," said the troll, "even if they want to root themselves into the ground." "All right!" cried Hans, driving the swine out of the yard. When he had followed them a short distance he met a couple of men who travelled about buying up cattle and swine. The men stopped and inquired whether these animals were for sale. "To be sure they are," replied Hans, "all except the old sow yonder She is intended for a present for our minister." Soon the price was fixed, and Hans received a sum of money, which he put into his pocket. When the two men had driven all the animals away, except the old sow, he took her to a marsh, where she soon buried herself in the mud, leaving only her tail above the ground. Hans, however, returned to the house. "What has become of the swine?" inquired the troll. "They went straight into the peat-bog, Master," answered Hans, "and they are all down there except the old sow, which I tried to stop. Her tail is yet above the ground, but all the rest of the animals are gone." The troll hastened along to the place, followed by Hans. Now the troll bent down, seized the sow's tail, and tried to pull her out. The tail slipped out of his hands, however, and he tumbled into the water. When he came out again he ran around furiously, trying to find his swine, but, as Hans said, they were already far away. "I hope that Master is not angry with me," said Hans. No, he was not at all angry, he asserted.

When the troll returned home he said to his wife : "How in the world can I get rid of this wretch? He will ruin and spoil our whole property. Oh, how I wish I could cool my rage upon him ! But I must keep our agreement, even if it costs all that I have." "I have an idea !" cried his wife. "I think I know how we may get rid of him. He knows that his time is up when the cuckoo begins to tune his voice. Of course it will be long before that time comes, but we may deceive him. You tar me and roll me in feathers until I look like a bird, then help me up into the large apple-tree, where I will cry,

"THE TAIL SLIPPED OUT OF HIS HANDS"

'Cuckoo, cuckoo!' until he thinks that the cuckoo has really come!" "You are a cunning woman," answered the troll, admiringly; "it shall be as you say." Upon this they retired, well pleased.

Next morning Hans and the troll were sitting at the breakfast-table—the woman was outside—when all at once they heard the cuckoo chant from the apple-tree, "Cuckoo, cuckoo!" "Listen!" said the troll; "the cuckoo has come." "I must see him," exclaimed Hans, jumping up and running out of the door; "I always used to have a look at the first cuckoo in the summer!" When he came into the garden he seized a sharp flint-stone and threw it at the head of the old woman, who was sitting in the tree cuckooing with all her might. She fell to the ground at once, stone dead. "Come, Master," called Hans, "come and look at this wonderful cuckoo!" The troll at once came running, and when he saw what had happened he began to curse and swear with such force that sparks flew from both of his eyes. "Master is not angry, I hope," said the boy. "You great scoundrel," yelled the troll, furiously, "yes, yes, I am! I am so furious, raving mad that I feel like bursting with rage! Now you know it. You sold my rye, you spoiled my horses and swine, and now you have killed my wife. Hoo, hoo, hoo!" and he was fairly shaking and trembling with fury.

"Well," said Hans, quietly, "we must deal with each other according to our agreement!" So he seized the troll and thrashed him until he was hardly able to stir. When this was done he walked into the house, took the bushel of dollars which was due him, returning home with it. He lived long and happily with his parents and his brothers, and they saw or heard no more of the troll.

THE BOY WHO WENT TO THE NORTHWIND

HERE was once an old woman who had an only son, and as she was very weak and old the boy went into the store-room to fetch the flour which she was to use for dinner. When he passed the staircase, however, the Northwind swept through the yard, carrying the flour away with him. The boy returned to the store-room for more, but the wind came again and swept it away, as before. When he came out the third time the wind again robbed him of his burden, carrying it away and spreading it over the fields and meadows. The boy now became very angry, and as he considered the treatment which he had suffered a shameful one, he decided to go to the Northwind and demand the article of which he had been robbed.

He started on his voyage, but, as the distance was very great, it took him a long time to reach his destination. At length he arrived at the dwelling of the Northwind.

"How do you do?" said the boy, "and thanks for the last time we were together!" "How are you?"

returned the Northwind—his utterance was thick—
"and thanks to yourself! What do you wish?"

"Well," answered the boy, "I wish you would be
good enough to return the flour of which you
robbed me when I was bringing it out of the store-
room. We have very little, and when you proceed
in this manner we must all starve." "I have no
flour," replied the wind, 'but since you are so poor
I will give you a table-cloth which will produce all
that you need as soon as you bid it thus : 'Cloth,
spread yourself, and bring the finest and best
dishes !' "

Now the boy was well contented ; but as the distance was too great to permit him to return in one
day, he stepped into an inn at the roadside, and,
when all the guests were ready for supper, he laid
the cloth on a table in the corner of the room, and
said : "Cloth, spread yourself, and bring the finest
and best dishes !" The words were hardly uttered
before the cloth was covered with all that they
could wish for, and every one thought that this
was an excellent treasure. This was especially the
thought of the innkeeper's wife, and in the night,
when all were asleep, she stole into the boy's room
and laid in its place another and similar cloth,
which was not capable, however, of producing even
an old bread-crust.

When the boy awoke he took his table-cloth and
pursued his way. Later in the day he arrived home.
"Well," he said, "I paid a visit to the Northwind.

He was a very good-natured fellow, and he gave me this table-cloth, which will produce the finest and best dishes as soon as you place it on the table, saying: 'Cloth, spread yourself, and bring the finest and best dishes!'" "Maybe," answered his mother, "but I shall not believe it until I see it done." Her son hastily pulled a table into the middle of the room, laid the cloth on it, and repeated the formula, without the least effect, however.

"I shall be obliged to go back to the Northwind," said the boy. He started at once, and in due time reached the place where the wind dwelt. "Good-evening!" said he, entering the house. "Good-evening!" cried the Northwind. "I wish to be paid for the flour of which you robbed me," continued the boy. "The table-cloth which I received is good for nothing." "I have no flour," answered the Northwind, "and all that I can give you is the old cane which stands in yonder corner. But if you say to it, 'Cane, strike!' it will strike on until you call, 'Cane, stop!' This cane I can give you."

As the distance was rather long, the boy, on his return home, stopped at the same inn where he had been before. As he suspected the innkeeper, however, of having stolen his table-cloth, he stretched himself on a bench and appeared to fall asleep, snoring loudly. The innkeeper, in the mean time, thought that no doubt the boy's cane possessed some wonderful power, and therefore prepared himself to replace it with another which looked exactly like it. As soon as he touched the cane, however, the boy shouted, "Cane, strike!" The cane at once began to dance upon the innkeeper's back, and with so good effect that he jumped around over tables and chairs, crying: "Make it stop, make it stop, for heaven's sake! If you don't, it 'll kill me! I will give you back your table-cloth!" When the boy thought the innkeeper had had enough, he said, "Cane, stop!" Seizing his cloth and thrusting it into his pocket, he walked away and returned home safe and sound.

The magic cloth proved to be good payment for the flour.

THERE were once a man and his wife who had an only son named Hans. It happened, as it has often happened with an only child, that he was petted and spoiled, and was not taught to obey. He was a reckless boy when small, and as he grew up he became more and more so. There was no tree and no house-top so high that he did not climb them.

Hans did not care to go to school and learn something useful, like other children, but he was so clever that he at once understood all that he heard or saw. There was no end to his pranks and jokes, and his best amusement was to frighten people, while he himself could not be frightened by anything in the world, man or beast.

As Hans grew up his parents thought that the time had come to teach him some manners, and have him kept in check, if possible. Although his mother doted upon him, his father brought him to the deacon, asking that worthy man to polish his manners the best he could. Were the deacon only able to frighten him in some manner, the father thought he would at length improve, but if he went into the world without respect or regard for any one, or anything, he would never fare well. The deacon promised to do his best, and the boy soon was initiated into his new duties.

One evening, at a rather late hour, the deacon said to him : "You must ring the bell to-night ; the ringer is drunk, and if you will do it I will give you eight pennies." "All right," answered the boy, whereupon he trudged across the church-yard and ascended the stairway in the dark steeple, and as he thought it great fun to ring the bells, he pulled the rope so vigorously that the sound was heard throughout the seven adjoining towns nps.

When the ringing was over, Hans descended the steps, but was stopped by a tall, white ghost which stood before him. "If you are alive, speak! If you are dead, begone !" shouted Hans. The ghost made no reply, but lifted its arm in a threatening manner. Hans now jumped forward, pushing the figure down the whole flight of steps. It rolled from one landing to another, and remained lying in the cellar at the bottom of the staircase. The boy paid no further attention to it, but went back to the deacon's house.

"Did you see any one?" asked his mistress. "Yes," replied Hans, "a tall, white ghost came and threatened me, but I ran against it and pushed it down the whole flight of steps." "Dear me!" cried the deacon's wife ; "I hope it was not hurt." "I don't

care," returned the boy, "whether it was or not."
She asked him, however, to follow her to the steeple,
and, although Hans thought she was too tender-
hearted, he complied. When they reached the cellar, there lay the deacon at the bottom of the staircase with one leg broken, and there they found the
white sheet which he had wrapped around himself
when he wanted to appear as a ghost and frighten
the boy. They carried him home and put him to
bed, but ever since that day the deacon carried a
lame leg. He did not wish to have anything more
to do with this reckless boy, but sent him home to
his parents, who were very angry because their son
had behaved so badly. His father now asked the
minister to take him into his service. " Yes ; let
him come," was the answer. "I shall manage to
knock the foolishness out of his head, depend upon
that." Thus Hans came to serve the minister.

One Saturday evening, towards midnight, Hans
was called out of bed by his master, who said to
him : "My son, I forgot my Bible at the altar in
the church last Sunday. Will you kindly go and
bring it back with you, as I must use it to-morrow
morning? I will give you twelve pennies for your
trouble."

Hans arose, seized the key which was handed him
by the minister, and went into the church. When
he reached the altar he noticed the Bible which lay
upon it ; but a tall, dark figure of a man was bending over it, reading. It was an easy matter to this

man to read in the dark, for his eyes gleamed like red fireballs. "Excuse me," said Hans, snatching the book out of his hands. Upon this he walked back to the door, locked it, and returned to the minister with the Bible and the key.

"Did you see anything remarkable?" asked his master. "No," answered the boy. "Oh yes; there was a tall, dark man reading in the book, but I merely said, 'Excuse me,' and seized it." "Were you not frightened?" pursued his master. "No," replied Hans; "why should I be frightened?" "You had better return home," said the minister; "I can teach you nothing."

Hans returned home and told what had happened. His father became furious, and said that when he feared neither the living nor the dead he did not wish to keep him at home. The next morning, consequently, Hans was obliged to go away, in spite of the pleading and the tears of his mother, who was afraid that he might not be able to fight his way in the great world of which he knew nothing. She followed him to the gate, kissed him, and said, with many tears, "God keep you, my poor boy!"

All the long day Hans pursued his way, and when it grew dark he walked into a church-yard, where weeping-willows could shield him until next morning. He lay down, but towards midnight he awoke and found an old man with a long beard bending over him. He carried a sickle in his right hand, and in his left an hour-glass. "Are you not afraid,"

"' EXCUSE ME,' SAID HANS"

asked Death—for he it was—"to lie here alone?"
"No," returned the boy, "what should I be afraid
of?" "You seem to be a brave boy," observed
Death. "Would you like to visit me?" "Yes;
where do you live?" answered Hans. "Directly
east of the church," explained his old friend; "where
you see a light shine from the ground, you will find
a hole. Descend through that, and come to-morrow night at this hour." Hans promised, and Death
parted from him.

He passed the following day in picking nuts about
the church-yard and in the adjoining woods. When
midnight came he entered the church-yard, and east
of the church he found what seemed to be an open
grave, through which a red glare was seen. As
there was no rope or ladder, Hans resolutely jumped into the opening. He fell a long distance, but
landed safely on a soft meadow. A few steps away
from him a door opened into a large building from
which the same ruddy glare issued, and in the doorway his old friend Death was standing, bidding him
welcome.

When they came into the house Hans noticed
that great numbers of lighted candles stood everywhere. There was a huge hall filled with them.
Some were as tall as church-candles, others were
of ordinary size, and there were some as small as
those which are used for Christmas-trees. Some
burned brightly, others feebly, and there were some
which seemed ready to go out. "Why do you burn

all these candles?" inquired Hans. "That is a part of my duty," replied the old man; "these are flames of the lives of all living beings. Whenever one goes out I must be on duty. You notice there are all sizes among them. Some are long yet, and some are short; some will soon have burned up, and they are the life-flames of those who must soon die. There is not one light but will some day burn out."

"Where is my candle?" inquired Hans again. Death showed him a tall and stately candle, which pleased the boy exceedingly. But when they came to look at his parents' candles, he found that of his father long and vigorous, while there was but little left of his mother's. He asked Death to be allowed to exchange them, and the request was granted. At length they arrived at an empty candlestick. The light was nearly extinguished; only a small spot of wax was left. "This was once a large candle," said Death, "but now it is nearly burned up. Because it has burned in God's service, there is great power in this bit of wax." He then told Hans how a king of a land far away had been paralyzed many years ago, and how he had promised his daughter's hand in marriage to the man who could cure him. The successful person was to receive one-half of the kingdom at once, and ascend the throne when he died. "Go there at once," concluded Death; "take service at the palace. You will be told never to name the king, for he has issued an edict that he who does so must either cure him or be hanged.

"'YOU SEEM TO BE A BRAVE BOY'"

When you see the king call his name aloud, and when you are told to cure him rub him with this wax. Be careful and keep it well. And now good-bye." Upon this Death conducted Hans to a door, which was opened and then closed behind him. He found himself in the church-yard at the very moment when the sun arose.

Hans now set out to find the land where the invalid king was living. All whom he asked told him that it was very far away. He walked on day and night, however, begging a bite of bread at the houses which he happened to pass.

When at length he had reached the palace, he walked in and offered his services. He was given a place among the grooms, and from the superintendent of the stables he received the warning never to name the king; if he did, he risked his life.

The sick king found pleasure in watching the watering of his horses; every day his easy-chair was rolled to one of the windows, 'rom which he had a view of the court-yard, and where he could sit and watch all his beautiful animals. One day, when Hans drove them to the fountain in the middle of the yard, he glanced towards the window, exclaiming: "Look, there is the king!" The other grooms bid him be silent, but the king having heard his words sent for the superintendent, whom he scolded for not giving his servants better instructions. "However," concluded he, "the law must be enforced. Bring the boy before me!"

When Hans was brought into the room the king said to him: "You know the law, and as you have dared, nevertheless, to utter my name, you must cure me, or lose your life. I suppose that death will be your fate, for you do not look wise enough to fulfil the other condition." Hans said that he wished to do his best, at any rate. Producing his wax he commenced rubbing the fingers of the king's right hand, which had been lame for many years. The king at once was able to move his fingers, whereupon the whole arm was rubbed with good effect. The king bid Hans rub away the lameness from the remainder of his body; but the boy replied that this could not be done until they had agreed upon his reward for curing the king entirely. He desired to have it in writing, with the king's own signature attached. The king, of course, must comply with his wishes, and as he felt quite generous he agreed, in writing, to give him the princess and one-half of the kingdom at once, neither more nor less. The remainder of the kingdom Hans was to inherit after the king's death. When the agreement had been signed the boy rubbed with the wax all over his body, and thus the king became healthy and well again.

By virtue of the agreement Hans was now a prince, and could, of course, wear nothing but a prince's dress. As soon as he had put on his new clothes he was conducted to the princess, who liked him so well that she had—as Hans had been expecting all the time — no objection to marrying him.

Their wedding was then celebrated in a truly Royal manner. Hans at once received one-half of the land, and began to rule it. When he was well-established in his new position he returned in a stately manner, with his beautiful bride, to his old home. He found his mother, who was by that time a widow, alive, and she was both pleased with and proud of her great son. When Hans had presented one of their poor relatives with the farm, he returned, with his wife and mother, to his new home. The old lady lived happily with her children. She witnessed both how Hans became king of the entire land when the old king had died, and how a number of sweet small princes and princesses learned, one after another, to love their "dear grandma."

NE day Fortune and Knowledge took a walk together. They happened to drift into a discussion as to what would be of the greatest benefit to mankind. Knowledge thought that to be possessed of a profound learning was most desirable; but Fortune maintained that good luck was the indispensable thing. "Do you see that dull-looking boy ploughing in yonder field?" asked Fortune. "Throw yourself upon him, and make him wise and learned; we shall see how far he progresses without my help."

The dull-looking boy at this moment stopped his horses, looked around, and said to an old man who was helping him that he felt he had become, all at once, so wise that there was nothing of which he did not know all that was or ever would be known. He needed no more to do such common work as ploughing, but wished to go to town and make his fortune by means of his great knowledge.

When he arrived in town he decided to take up a watch-maker's trade. So he entered the house of the Royal watch-maker, asking for a place as an ap-

"FORTUNE AND KNOWLEDGE TOOK A WALK TOGETHER"

prentice in the workshop. "No," said the watch-maker, "your hands are too big and rough for this kind of work, and you look as if you were able to play a good knife and fork." The young man plead-ed as best he could, however, and at length he of-fered the watch-maker a hundred dollars if he would give him the place he desired. There was now no objection on the part of the master; the young man had his will, but asked to be allowed to work in a room by himself. This was not granted, however, and at length he was given a place among the other apprentices.

The first piece of work which he was asked to do was the polishing of the face of a tower-clock; such toil seemed the most suitable for his big hands. Both this and all other work which he undertook was done, however, to the satisfaction of his master.

One day the king sent a message to the watch-maker, bidding him to make a clock which could walk about on the table, all by itself. When the king said, "Here sits the king!" it was to stop in front of his seat, and beat. This clock was to be finished at a certain time in the near future.

The watch-maker became much puzzled, and said that it was impossible to fulfil his majesty's wish; but the king told him that unless he obeyed his privilege would be taken away from him and given to some one else.

The poor man was much perplexed by this order but his new apprentice asked to be allowed to make the clock. No attention was paid to this offer, however, and when it was repeated he received a sharp rebuke. As his master looked more and more dejected he offered his services for the third time, and was finally allowed to make the trial ; moreover, he was given a room by himself in order that he might remain undisturbed.

When he had been working for some time his master entered to see how he was getting on. "Look, master !" said the young man, "these are the drawings for the clock. The plans are ready, so that the real work can begin." "Let me see once," replied his master, putting on his glasses. He looked from the floor to the ceiling, and back again, and wherever he looked he saw the most singular figures and drawings. "Yes," he said, at length, "this looks well enough ;" whereupon he walked away. When he stepped into the room, a month later, the apprentice said to him : "All the wheels and other pieces are now ready ; when they have been put together the clock is finished." He showed him all these things, and his master could not help thinking, "What will come of it all?" He said nothing, however, but only nodded, and hastened away.

A short time afterwards he returned. At the door he was met by his apprentice, who said : "Now, master, the clock is finished, and we will try it !" "Yes," answered the old man, eagerly ; "let us try it !" The clock was placed on the table, at one end of which the master seated himself. The clock walked about, indeed, and when the master, who played the king's part, addressed it, saying, " Here sits the king," it stopped in front of him and beat the exact time. The watch-maker was delighted, and the little clock was obliged to walk about to amuse him and all his apprentices.

On the appointed day the Royal watch-maker appeared at the palace with the clock, followed by his apprentice. The clock was tried in the presence of the whole court, and did its duty so well that the king was not only pleased but wondered greatly at the skill with which the work had been done. He asked his watch-maker why he had been at first so puzzled and so afraid of undertaking the work, since he had been able, nevertheless, to carry it out so well. Thus the man was obliged to explain that it was not he but the boy who had done the work. When the king learned this he declared that if the young man had been able to make this clock he deserved to be promoted. The old man was not satisfied with this declaration, as the boy's apprenticeship was not yet up. When the king gave him, however, a hundred dollars he hesitated no more but did it readily.

The same king had a daughter whom no one could induce to utter a single word. Her father was much afflicted, and promised to make the one who could induce her to speak his successor and

son-in-law. Those who tried and failed must, however, lose their lives.

Many persons from all parts of the country had
tried in vain to restore the young lady's power of
speech. One by one they were conducted into the
room of the princess, but no one could call forth a
single sound from her by way of reply.

At length the watch-maker's apprentice decided
to try, so this young man, whom Knowledge had endowed so well, entered the room. He affected not
to see the princess at all, but walked up to a mirror
hanging there, and addressed it thus : "Good-morning, little mirror ! Let me tell you a story ! There
were once three men who walked about in the
country : a tailor, a sculptor, and a teacher. As
they were obliged to keep up a fire at night, they
decided that one of them must always keep awake,
while the two others slept. First the sculptor was
to watch—but this is merely a story, little mirror !—
and when he ꙡoked about in the dark, he found an
infant boy in the grass. He was so surprised that
he awoke the tailor, and while the latter rubbed his
eyes—but this is merely a tale, little mirror !—he
sewed a whole dress for the child. When the school-
master's turn came, he at once taught the little boy
to speak. But to which of these three men did this
boy belong, little mirror ?"

"It belonged to the sculptor, of course, since he
found it," said the princess, who had become so in-
terested in the story that she could not help an-

IN THE HANGMAN'S HANDS

nouncing her opinion. The young man nodded to the mirror, saying: "That is right, little mirror; thanks to you for your kindness!" Upon this he walked out of the door without even looking at the princess. The ministers, however, who had been listening outside, having heard nothing, took him into the court-yard to be hanged. At the very same moment the king happened to pass the yard, and as soon as he saw whom the hangman had in his hands, and recognized him as the watch-maker's apprentice who had made the wonderful clock, he pardoned him at once.

Some time afterwards the boy again tried to make the princess speak, but without succeeding—that is, the generals who were this time listening at the door declared that they heard nothing. The young man was accordingly taken into the court-yard and again doomed to be hanged.

At the same moment Fortune and Knowledge happened to pass outside. When they saw what was in progress they stopped. "Look!" exclaimed Fortune; "what good did his great wisdom do him? Now you must admit that fortune is far more valuable than knowledge" "Yes," replied Knowledge; "now you must help him if you can!" Fortune did so, for at the very moment when the young man was standing on the ladder, the princess rushed into the court-yard and told all: *He* had restored her power of speech; *him* she wanted to marry! Thus the young man escaped death, married the princess, and became king of the land.

THE SUITOR

HERE was once a handsome young fellow by the name of Tom. From an old, wealthy uncle he had inherited a fine farm, and being well established in life, he determined to seek a wife. As he was quite wealthy, he considered himself able to afford a little more than ordinary people in this direction, for the wives of wealthy men must always be prettier and wiser than those of the poor, as we all know.

So Tom wanted a wife who was handsome and industrious, wise and good, and of course it would not be out of the way if she possessed some property.

One day he rode over to a rich farmer who lived in the neighborhood, and who had three daughters, all of whom were ready to be married at once. He had seen, although he had never talked with, them, and thought well of all three.

Now these girls, who were otherwise pretty and good, had one great fault—namely, that they could not talk distinctly. When Tom came riding into the yard the farmer received him kindly, and conducted him into the room, where the three girls sat spinning diligently. They nodded kindly to him and smiled, but did not utter a sound, as their mother had strictly forbidden them to do so. The farmer led the talking, while his wife waited on them with good food and drinks. The girls spun and looked at the young man at the table, and glanced at each other and at the ceiling and out of the windows, but none of them spoke. At length the one happened to break her yarn. "My 'arn bote!" exclaimed she. "Tie it adain," advised her sister. "Mamma told us we say no'tin', and now we t'ant teep 'till!" broke in the third one.

When Tom heard these grown girls talk like babies, he hurried away, utterly shocked. A wife who could not speak distinctly he had no use for at all.

He proceeded to another farm, where they had a daughter who was said to be a very fine girl in all respects. Tom went into the house and saw her. If the first three ones had been too silent, this one talked, however, more fluently and volubly than any girl whom he had ever met. She talked like a house on fire, while her spinning-wheel went more rapidly than any engine. "How long does it take you to use up such a head of flax?" asked the young man, pointing to the rock. "Oh," she said, "I use up a couple of them every day."

While she left the room a few minutes to look after the servants, Tom seized a key from a drawer of a bureau in the room and stuffed it into the head of flax. When she returned, they finished their conversation ; whereupon he bid her parents and herself good-bye, promising to call again in a week.

On the appointed day Tom returned. The girl and her parents expected him to talk this time of his errand. When he came into the room the girl was busy with her rock, as before. She bid him welcome, and invited him to sit down. " How unfortunate !" began she. "We have been missing the key of that bureau ever since you were here. We are unable to find it, and I cannot reach any of my things. It never happened before."

On hearing this, Tom went over and pulled the key out of the head of flax. It was the same key, and, still worse, the very same head of flax that he had seen a week before. Thus he knew her word could not be depended upon ; and bidding her good-bye he left at once, richer in experience than before.

Some time afterwards he heard of a girl who was very pretty and good, but especially wise and thoughtful in all practical matters. Her parents were said to be the same. Tom saddled his horse and rode over to see her.

The whole family was at home, and received the young man very kindly. While the men drifted into a talk about the weather and crops, the women placed before them the best that the house could afford. " Go into the cellar and fetch a bottle of wine," said the woman to her daughter. The girl went into the cellar, but was so busy thinking what pattern she might choose for a wedding-dress that she sat down on the floor, lost in reflection upon this important subject, and the wine was entirely forgotten.

After she had left the room, the parents told Tom of their daughter's many good qualities; how industrious she was, how thoughtful, and so on. The young man thought that she would be exactly such a wife as he wished. But as the girl did not appear with the wine, her mother went to see what had become of her. When she came into the cellar, and found her daughter sitting on the floor, she asked: "Why do you sit there, instead of bringing the wine?" "Well," was the answer, "I am thinking that if I marry Tom I must make a careful choice of the pattern for my wedding-gown. The question is, what pattern would do best?" "Yes, indeed," answered her mother, "which pattern *will* be the most suitable?" She sat down by her daughter, pondering over this important question.

"I wonder what has become of them both!" at length exclaimed the man, referring to his wife and daughter. "I must look after them." He went into the cellar, and when he saw both women sitting on the floor, he cried: "Why are you both sitting here? You have kept us waiting for over an hour!" "We are thinking," replied his wife, "of the pattern for the wedding-gown. If she is to marry Tom, the gown must, of course, be a pretty one, and the choice of the right pattern is, indeed, an important matter."

"To be sure!" answered her husband, seating himself on the floor beside them to consider the same subject.

As at length Tom grew tired of waiting, he went himself into the cellar to see if anything unusual had happened. He found the whole family sitting on the floor and looking extremely thoughtful. "Why do you all sit here?" he asked. At length the farmer, aroused from his reverie, proceeded to relate the difficult question which had caught their attention.

"Yes, in-dee-e-ed," answered Tom. "Which will be the most suitable pattern? You may think of that until I return, and in the mean time I will do the same. Good-bye to you!"

Mounting his horse, he rode home as rapidly as the steed would carry him, and if he has not found another and less thoughtful girl, he is yet a bachelor.

But the three people may yet be sitting on the cellar floor, thinking of the pattern for the bridal gown, for all that I know!

HERE was once a poor man who walked about in the woods gathering fuel. His wife and children at home were in want of all that was necessary both to bite and to burn. As he moved about the trees picking up the dead branches, a stranger came along, who stopped and addressed him. When the poor man told of his miserable condition, and how he could not, even by the hardest work, procure the necessities of life for nimself, his wife, and children, the stranger said: " Indeed ! That is a dog's life ; but it will depend upon yourself whether or not your conditions be improved—I may assist you. If you are willing to give me the first thing that you see when you reach your hut, I shall see that you are provided with all that you need for the rest of your lifetime."

The man considered this proposition a moment. "What I see first," thought he, "is generally the old jack in the clearing in front of the house. He may have that, if he cares; I can easily make another." So he closed the bargain, and they separated.

The poor man approached his house, thinking how well it would be when all the small mouths, which were so often clamoring for bread, could be filled with good things, and the little cheeks become as rosy-red as they ought to have been long ago. He stooped forward, bending his head under the heavy burden of the fagots, when suddenly a merry voice called : " Papa—there is papa !" Lifting his head and glancing in the direction of his house, he saw his youngest boy rush along the path to meet him. There was no time to warn the child or keep him back ; he had seen him first, and of course he must part with him. It gave him great pain ; but when he entered the house and found abundance of everything he appeared cheerful and unconcerned, and said nothing of the promise which the stranger had received from him.

Time passed. The man expected every day to lose his child, but no one came. The little boy gradually developed a wonderful keenness and scholarship. In school he could be taught nothing that he did not already know, so at length he was allowed to stay at home, where he read and wrote diligently, paying visits to both the blacksmith and the minister—the two learned men in this part of the country — who loaned him all sorts of queer books.

On his thirteenth birthday the boy told his father that he knew all about the agreement with the man in the forest. " Now you must take a knife and

"THAT IS A DOG'S LIFE."

carve a three-legged chair and a three-legged table
for me. The man to whom you sold me was the
Evil One, who has already prepared a seat for me
in his dwelling. You must use no other tool than a
knife, and have the two articles ready before my
next birthday. The Evil One's table and chair will
become smaller and smaller as you carve mine,
and when your work is finished they will have vanished entirely."

His father at once went to work, cutting and
carving diligently, and when the year came round
the chair and the table were finished. On the boy's
fourteenth birthday the two went into the woods.
Here the boy made a circle on the earth, bidding
his father seat himself within it, for as long as he
stayed there no one could hurt a hair of his head,
and if he remained there one whole day he would
be free—the Evil One would have no power over
him.

" It is much more difficult with me," said the boy,
"although the Evil One cannot cross the circle
which I shall draw around myself. I must stay
there until a beautiful maiden is willing to save
me. She must come and carry me away with her;
but until the news of my fate can reach the world,
and she can be found, I must stay within the circle, otherwise I shall become the property of the
Enemy."

Leaving his father in the circle which he had
drawn around him he went away a short distance

and drew another, placing the table and the chair within it; and seating himself on the chair, he read diligently in a book which he had placed on the table before him. Soon Lucifer came walking along. The man had not known him before, but this time he was in no doubt as to who he was.

Stopping near the father, the Enemy said: "Now the time has come for you to fulfil your part of the agreement." "Go and take the boy, if you can," replied the man; "I have brought him along. He is not far away." Lucifer went to the boy, stopped near the circle, and said: "Come here! You belong to me." "Take me, if you can," was the answer. The Evil One reached after him, but to no effect; he could not grasp him, and it was impossible for him to cross the circle. At length he returned to the father, and tried to coax and scare him away from his retreat, but all in vain; and when he had run back and forth between the two for a considerable length of time, he finally lost his patience and walked away. In twenty-four hours the father was at liberty to leave his circle and return home; but the boy remained where he was, awaiting the time when a beautiful maiden should come and save him.

At length, as the news of his cruel fate reached far and wide, a fair young princess who lived in a palace south of the sun, west of the moon, and in the middle of the wind, determined to rescue him. She came driving in a golden carriage, stopped in the forest where the boy sat reading, and told him to enter and sit beside her. He complied, and away they drove—far away from the place where the Enemy had played his pranks. When they arrived at the wonderful palace south of the sun, west of the moon, and in the middle of the wind, he received a place among her servants, and finding him both good and true, she determined to marry him.

The young man could not, however, forget his old home. He told his fair young princess that if she would allow him to return for a short time to see how his parents were, he would be better prepared to live far away from them during the rest of his lifetime. He was longing to see his mother once more ; no doubt she missed him and shed many tears for his sake, thinking that she would never see him again. The princess was pleased, and said : "It shall be as you desire. I will bring you home, and you may stay there until you long for me. Take this ring ; when you wish to return, turn it ; but do not wish me to come to you. In that case we shall both become unhappy !" Upon this they entered the golden carriage again, and drove on as rapidly as thoughts can travel, until they reached the small hut in the forest. As soon as the young man alighted the carriage disappeared, and had not the ring been gleaming on his finger he would have thought it all a dream.

When he entered his old home his parents were much astonished to see him ; they had, of course, thought him dead long ago. He told them what had happened and how well he had fared, and they wondered much at his good fortune. It was their greatest desire to see the fair princess who had rescued him, and they were never tired of asking him to call her, that they might themselves thank and admire her. He answered again and again that this could not be—that the princess had forbidden it. As they could not restrain their desire, however, and as he was himself anxious to see her, he at length turned the ring on his finger, wishing her to come. At once the princess appeared, snatched the ring away from him, boxed his ears effectively, and vanished as rapidly as she had come. Now he stood there, deprived of his happiness and all means of returning to her.

As he could not remain at home he bid his parents good-bye, and set out to seek his lost happiness. He walked a long distance, and at length lost his way entirely. One day, when he stopped to rest in the depths of a large forest, he noticed a couple of kobolds quarrelling about something. "What are you quarrelling about?" asked he. Well, they had found a pair of slippers which would enable their owner to cover ten miles in one step. Each of them wanted these, and each said that he had found them. "No use to quarrel about that," said the young man. "Each of you may take one and cover ten miles in *two* steps." But such a plan did not suit them. "Well," said the young man again,

"THE PRINCESS RECEIVED HIM GRACEFULLY"

"I propose that you race as far as the large stone yonder. He who returns first may have the slippers." They agreed upon this, and started, raising the dust like a cloud behind them. When they returned they found the young man and the slippers had both disappeared. The kobolds looked at each other, and were sensible enough to understand that this was the easiest way in which to settle the dispute.

The young man now rapidly pursued his way. Towards evening he stopped at the gate of a large and magnificent palace. Upon his inquiry who lived there, he was told that the Wind-king was the owner of this stately mansion. "No doubt," thought he, "the Wind-king can tell me where the palace south of the sun, west of the moon, and in the middle of the wind is situated." He entered and requested an audience of the king. When taken into his presence and inquiring about the palace which he was seeking, he was told by his majesty that the location of the place was altogether unknown to him. Towards evening all the winds were, however, to return home. He, the king, would ask if any of them knew of such a place as the palace south of the sun, west of the moon, and in the middle of the wind. Some one of them would be likely to know.

Towards evening there was a whistling and howling around the palace, and when all the winds had taken their seats in the large hall, the king entered, inquiring if all were there. Some one replied that the Northwest had not yet arrived, but that he must soon come. A few minutes afterwards the Northwest came howling through the gate, pushed the doors open, and fell into his seat with a loud crack. "Do you know a palace which is located south of the sun, west of the moon, and in the middle of the wind?" inquired the king. All shook their heads except the Northwest, who nodded gravely and gloomily, and said that he had passed it occasionally; but it was very, very far away. The king now told him to carry a young man with him the next morning, but the wind replied that a young man who could only walk on the ground would never reach the place; he himself could not carry such a burden; it would detain him too much, and he would never reach the end of his journey. The king replied, however, that there was no help for it; he was to take the young man along with him the next morning whether he wished to or not.

Next morning the Northwest looked if possible still more gloomy than the evening before; he did not like to keep company with a walking person, but as the king's orders must be obeyed, he moved very slowly in order to keep pace with his companion. The latter was, however, very soon so far ahead that the wind was obliged to quicken his steps considerably; but the farther they came the more rapidly he had to move, and at length he be-

came a tremendous tempest. About noontime
they reached the palace, but the Northwest had
become so tired that he was obliged to rest under
a tree while the young man put off the slippers.
He walked the last part of the way without slippers,
otherwise he would have passed without seeing it.

When he entered the palace the princess received
him gleefully She had never dared to think that
he would ever be able to reach her again. Their
wedding was celebrated in a gorgeous manner, and
they are living yet, happy and contented, in their
beautiful palace south of the sun, west of the moon,
and in the middle of the wind.

 MAN and his wife were once living in a very small cottage—the smallest and most ill-looking hut in the whole village. They were very poor, and often wanted even daily bread. Somehow or other they had managed to keep an only cow, but had been obliged to sell nearly everything else that they had. At length they decided that the cow, too, must go, and the man led her away, intending to bring her to the market. As he walked along the road a stranger approached and hailed him, asking if he intended to sell the animal, and how much he would take for it.

"I think," answered he, "that twenty dollars would be a fair price."

"Money I cannot give you," resumed the stranger, "but I have something which is worth as much as twenty dollars. Here is a pot which I am willing to give for your cow." Saying this, he pulled forth an iron pot with three legs and a handle.

"A pot !" exclaimed the cow's owner. "What use would that do me when I have nothing to put in it? My wife and children cannot eat an iron pot. No; money is what I need, and what I must have."

The two men stood still a moment looking at each other and at the cow and the pot, when suddenly the three-legged being began to speak. "Just take me," said it. When the poor man heard this he thought that if it could speak no doubt it could do more than that. So he closed the bargain, received the pot, and returned home with it.

When he reached his hut he first went to the stall where the cow had been standing, for he did not dare to appear before his wife at once. Having tied the pot to the manger, he went into the room, asking for something to eat, as he was hungry from his long walk. "Well," said his wife, "did you make a good bargain at the market? Did you get a good price for the cow?" "Yes," he said, "the price was fair enough." "That is well," returned she. "The money will help us a long time." "No," said he, again, "I received no money for the cow." "Dear me!" cried she. "What did you receive, then?" He told her to go and look in the stall.

As soon as the woman learned that the three-legged pot was all that had been paid him for the cow, she scolded and abused him. "You are a great blockhead!" cried she. "I wish I had myself taken the cow to the market! I never heard of such foolishness!" Thus she went on for a while.

"Clean me and put me on the fire," suddenly shouted the pot.

The woman opened her eyes in great wonder, and now it was her turn to think that if the pot could talk no doubt it could do more than this. She cleaned and washed it carefully and put it on the fire.

"I skip, I skip!" cried the pot.

"How far do you skip?" asked the woman.

"To the rich man's house, to the rich man's house!" it cried again, running from the fireplace to the door, across the yard, and up the road, as fast as the three short legs would carry it. The rich man lived not very far away. His wife was engaged in baking bread when the pot came running in and jumped up on the table, where it remained standing quite still. "Ah," exclaimed the woman, "isn't it wonderful! I just needed you for a pudding which must be baked at once." Thus she heaped a great many good things into the pot—flour, sugar, butter, raisins, almonds, spices, and so on. The pot received it all with a good will. At length the pudding was made, but when the rich man's wife reached for it, intending to put it on the stove, tap, tap, tap went the three short legs, and the pot stood on the threshold of the open door. "Dear me, where are you going with my pudding?" cried the woman. "To the poor man's home," rep.ied the pot, running down the road at great speed.

When the poor people saw the pot coming back,

and found the pudding, they rejoiced, and the man lost no time in asking his wife whether the bargain did not seem to be an excellent one after all. Yes, she was quite pleased and contented.

Next morning the pot again cried: "I skip, I skip!" "How far do you skip?" asked they.

"To the rich man's barn!" it shouted, running up the road. When it arrived at the barn it stopped in the door. "Look at that black pot!" cried the men, who were threshing wheat. "Let us see how much it will hold." They poured a bushel of wheat into it, but it did not seem to fill rapidly. Another bushel went in, but there was still room. Now every grain of wheat went into the pot, but still it seemed capable of holding much more. As there was no more wheat to be found, the three short legs began to move, and when the men looked around the pot had reached the gate. "Stop, stop!" called they. "Where do you go with our wheat?" "To the poor man's home," replied the pot, speeding down the road and leaving the men behind, dismayed and dumfounded.

The poor people were delighted when they received wheat enough to feed them for several years.

On the third morning the pot again skipped up the road. It was a beautiful day. The sun shone so bright and pleasant that the rich man had spread his money on a table near the open window to prevent his gold from becoming mouldy. All at once

the pot stood on the table before him. He began
to count his money over, as wealthy men sometimes
like to do, and although he could not imagine where
this black pot had come from, he thought it would
be a good place to keep his money in the future.
So he threw in one handful after another until it
held all. At the same moment the pot made a
jump from the table to the window-sill. "Wait!"
shouted he. "Where do you go with all my money?"
"To the poor man's home," returned the pot, skip-
ping down the road until the money danced within
it. In the middle of the floor in the poor man's hut
it stopped, making its owners cry out in rapture
over the unexpected treasure. "Clean and wash
me," said the pot, "and put me aside."

Next morning it again announced that it was
ready to skip.

"How far do you skip?" asked they.

"To the rich man's house!" So it ran up the
road again, never stopping until it had reached the
wealthy people's kitchen. The man happened to
be there himself this time, and as soon as he saw it
he cried: "There is the pot which carried away
our pudding, our wheat, and all our money! I
shall make it return what it stole!" He flung himself upon it, but found that he was unable to get off
again. "I skip, I skip!" shouted the pot. "Skip
to the north pole, if you wish!" yelled the man,
furiously, trying in vain to free himself. The three
short legs at once moved on, carrying him rapidly

down the road. The poor people saw it pass their
door ; but it never thought of stopping. For all
that I know, it went straight to the north pole with
its burden.

The poor people became wealthy, and often
thought of the wonderful pot with the three short
legs which skipped so cheerfully for their good. It
was gone, however, and they have never seen it
since it carried the rich man towards the north
pole.

MONEY WILL BUY EVERYTHING

HERE was once a soldier who stood sentry at a great man's house. As he grew tired from standing there alone, and wished to occupy himself in some way, he secured a piece of chalk and began to write on the house-wall. Whatever came into his mind he wrote down without giving much thought to it: there was no one to talk with, and writing was better than nothing. The by - passers read the words occasionally, but also without thinking much about them. One day the soldier wrote upon the wall: "Money will buy everything." Many saw and read it; some smiled and some frowned. At length an officer stopped in front of the wall. "Who wrote that?" asked he. The soldier answered that the writing was his work. "We shall see," observed the officer, "if you are able to prove your words!" Now he told all his friends of the soldier's act, and soon every one was talking about the words which he had written on the wall. At length it reached the king's ear; he put on his crown, gathered his purple cloak

THE WRITING ON THE WALL.

around him, and set out to see it with his own eyes.

"How dare you," said he to the soldier, "write this when you cannot prove it?" "Money *will* buy everything," replied the soldier.

The king became excited, and said again : "You *shall* prove what you say, upon my word! Take all the money you need from my treasury, and if you can prove your words within two years you may marry my daughter, but if you cannot you shall lose your life. I will lock her up so securely that no one can enter her room. If you can manage, by means of gold, to open the doors and talk with her, I shall believe what you wrote on the wall."

There the soldier stood, realizing that he was in a sad scrape. There was nothing to do, however, but to try his best, for the king had given the order, and it was useless to evade it. If he did nothing he would be hanged; such was the king's decree, and kings always keep their word.

The princess was now placed in a firm tower built of rocks, and her father told her to stay there until the two years had passed. There was only one small window in the room where she lived, and no one but the king possessed the key of the iron-clad door behind which she sat.

Time passed, and the soldier determined to do something. He went into the treasury, and took all the gold and silver that he was able to carry with him. Then he left the town and walked out into the wide world.

One night he lost his way in a large forest, but seeing a light at a distance he walked towards it, and reached a small house where an old woman lived quite alone. The soldier asked her for a night's lodging, and was allowed to sleep in the hay up in the loft. As they fell to talking he told the good old woman how he was situated: that within two years he must marry the princess or lose his life ; that he had enough money, but unless he knew what to do with it his riches were of little use to him.

"I think I can give you some advice," said the old woman. "Have a golden stag made, and let it be large enough to hold yourself. When it is finished creep into it, and hire some one to take it around and display it." She told him exactly how to proceed. Next morning the soldier bid the kind old woman good-bye, and pursued his way.

In the next town at which he arrived he engaged a jeweller to make a golden stag. It was to be large enough to hold him, and was to have a door on the one side in order that he might go in and out. His orders were promptly executed, and the door was so ingeniously concealed that no one could detect the slightest trace thereof. The soldier was much pleased with it, and paid a large sum of money to the skilful jeweller, whereupon he hired a man to display it, crept through the door, and closed it

after him, bidding the man to start for the Royal
residence.

The soldier had a great talent for music; he
possessed a fine voice, and this he made use of the
best he knew, while the man drew him along from
one place to another. Every one stopped and listened—a golden stag which sang so beautifully they
had never seen before. At length they passed the
Royal palace. When the king learned the news of
the singing stag, he came out to look at it, and was
much pleased to hear that it could sing all the tunes
which he liked best. He took such a fancy to the
stag that he wished to buy it; but the man, who
had received instructions from the soldier, asked
such a large sum that the king declared the pur-
chase impossible.

The princess had seen the stag from her window
and heard its beautiful voice. When her father
came into her room she besought him to buy it:
she had been sitting alone in the dreadful tower
for over a year, and the stag would help to cheer
her solitude. The king thought this wish reasonable enough, and finally bought the stag, which was
taken into the tower. The princess was happy, and
as soon as she wished for a song the stag readily
complied.

Towards evening, when the king had left his
daughter, the soldier opened the door and jumped
out. The princess was frightened, and began to
scream at the top of her voice. No one heard her,

however, and very soon the young man had explained all. He was very hungry, he said, and
when he had eaten a little he would hide himself
again. The next day she was to ask the king to remove the stag, and when this was done he would
come out from his hiding-place and tell her father
that money had opened her door for him in spite
of the locks and bolts

The king thought, in the mean time, that it would
be pleasant to hear one more tune from the wonderful stag before retiring for the night. So he entered the tower, and as he walked on tiptoe in
order to disturb no one, neither his daughter nor
the soldier heard his steps. They heard his *voice*,
however, when he came in and found how the soldier had managed to pass the bolted doors. "You
shall pay for this!" cried he, furiously , and forgetting himself entirely, he drew his golden sword, intending to kill the bold intruder. The soldier said,
quietly but firmly · "My dear king! Money opened
the doors for me in spite of your decrees. Keep
your word, and give me your daughter's hand in
marriage!" His majesty was obliged, of course, to
do this, so the soldier married the princess, and
needed no more to stand sentry or write on the
house-wall.

N his table in a poorly furnished room a little tailor was sitting. He sewed busily, while the flies buzzed about the window‑panes, and the beautiful sunshine gleamed bright and pleasant on the blooming elder-bushes and the rosy-red, shining cherries outside the house Under the eaves numerous sparrows were twittering cheerily

The door was opened and in came our tailor's friend, the blacksmith, dressed in his best coat, and with a knotty stick in his hand. "Do you sit there yet?" asked he. 'Do you not intend to visit the fair, like other good Christians?"

"I don't care to go," returned the tailor, in his faint, shrill voice

"How about your wife?" asked the blacksmith, again

"She went away more than two hours ago," answered he.

"Come, come, that beats all!" cried his friend. "Do you care so little for your clever little wife that you let her trudge to the fair alone on such a

day as this, when the roads are filled with vaga-
bonds and robbers?"

"My wife is in good hands," declared the tailor,
"for our wealthy neignbor, Mads, promised to take
care of her, and—"

"—And in the mean time you are forced to prick
with your needle this whole splendid summer day!"

"A tailor must attend to his duties," said the
shrivelled little fellow, looking helplessly into the
blacksmith's large face with the blinking eyes and
the curly beard. "When I was a boy I dreamed
of becoming a great warrior. I was to win a golden
helmet and ride on a stately steed, followed by a
hundred brave men. Nothing ever came of it!"

"Why should you not yet live to see your dream
realized?" pursued his friend, and nodded smilingly
at him.

"I know one thing!" cried the tailor, straighten-
ing himself and striking his breast. "I possess a
lion's courage and the force of a bear. Blood cannot frighten me! How often have I pricked my
fingers with a needle without feeling either fear or
pain! And oh, how I yet dream! Often I slay
dragons and serpents and other fearful beasts, the
very names of which would frighten you."

"Were I in your place," answered the blacksmith,
"I would at once throw these rags aside and jump
from the table, go into the wide world, seek those
great monsters you spoke of, and slay them—*slay
them!*"

"A LITTLE TAILOR WAS SITTING"

"No, no," replied the little man, "I cannot! At present I own not a single penny, and without money you can do nothing."

"I will aid you," returned the blacksmith. "Five dollars are all that I have, but I will share them with you, my friend. Two dollars and fifty cents will reach far in a thrifty man's hand. Come and take them!"

"My wife will feel very lonely," objected the tailor.

"Your wife! Mads and I will take care of her while you are gone," asserted his friend.

"Will you, surely?" asked the ambitious young man.

"I promise you solemnly!" cried the animated blacksmith. "Think of the day when you return with a golden helmet, and followed by a hundred great warriors!"

"Yes! yes!" shouted the tailor, slapping the table with his hand and sweeping the goods he had been at work with into a corner. "When I strike, I strike hard!" He lifted his hand and looked at it. When it struck the table seven flies had been killed, and their dead bodies stuck to the palm.

"Seven of them," said he, looking sternly at his friend. "Seven with one blow. Such is the beginning. What do you think of that?"

"Remarkable!" answered the blacksmith—"remarkable, indeed! Make a belt and sew on it, with red worsted, 'Seven with one Blow.' This will tell every one what a great man you are, and that is very important."

" I will follow your advice," returned the little tailor, " for now I am determined !"

In the afternoon he set out to win all that he had dreamed of. A short distance from home he met his wife and wealthy Mads, who returned from the market, laughing and talking about the fine day which had been passed so pleasantly. " Let her be glad and happy," thought the good little tailor, as they passed without seeing him ; " when I return she will be still more delighted." He walked on, the hopeful and trustful little person he was.

At the fair he met an old invalid soldier who had lost both of his arms in war, for which reason he had no more use for his weapons. The tailor bought his sword. It was rusty and hacked, but one dollar was a low price, and he was satisfied.

He pursued his way, well equipped and hopeful. Every one gave him shelter and food when needed, for the sake of the words which he had sewed on his belt, but when he inquired about dragons and serpents they shook their heads ; no such monsters were living in this part of the world. At length he began to doubt the many descriptions which he had read about these beings, and hesitated to believe the frightful havoc which they were said to have made.

Soon he heard, however, that in a country called Franconia there were many of these marvellous animals. As soon as one of them had been killed, another appeared, and they spared neither kings nor emperors. So this was a great country for the tailor, who went there without delay.

One evening he lay down to sleep in a large forest, and when he awoke the next morning he found two strangers in beautiful clothes staring at him. They read the inscription on his belt, and although un-acquainted with the language, succeeded in inter-preting the meaning of the words. Thinking of seven men, and not of seven flies, they approached the mighty hero, bowing and scraping, asking him to accompany them to the king and be enlisted in the Royal body-guard.

The king received the tailor well. "My people are a nation of heroes," said he; "we know how to value bravery. Soon you will have occasion to show your proficiency and your manhood."

The tailor replied that he was pleased to hear this, and that his greatest desire was to kill dragons and serpents. "In that case," said the king, "you may make a beginning by going into the forest behind this palace. Two fearful giants dwell there, and none of my heroes are as yet able to slay them They devour the entire crop, and at length they will lay the whole country waste. If you can slay them I will give you a hundred pieces of gold."

The little man's heart swelled within him, he beat his old rusty sword, and declared that even if there were seven giants, he would kill them as easily as if they were seven flies. He was conducted to the pantry, and received a large parcel containing ten whole slices of bread-and-butter. The queen had herself prepared them, and there were five with collared beef and five with sweet-milk cheese.

Thus equipped the tailor departed. When he had walked about in the forest a couple of hours without noticing even a trace of the giants, he determined to open the package and taste the dainty bread-and-butter. He had hardly swallowed the first bite before the leaves began to rattle, and in the next moment two huge men, fearful to look at, stood before him. They were so tall that if they had been standing on the stone stair in front of the tailor's hut it would have been an easy matter for them to look down into the chimney-top. Now his heart sank within him, and he dropped his bread-and-butter. "I wish to God," thought he, "that I had stayed among my needles and rags. Now I am a lost man."

So he was, indeed. The one giant seized him by the collar, and without even attempting an excuse, lifted him up, holding him out at arm's-length.

"Let us chop him in a trough and sprinkle him with pepper and salt; he will make a delicious supper," said one.

"He looks too withered and dry," answered his comrade. "We had better hang him up, dry, and stretch him. Why, such a shrivelled little creature can be better used for making bow-strings!"

"No ; let us eat him," proposed the other.

"We will dry him, as I said," returned his companion.

"Will we, indeed ?" replied the first, stealing a glance at his friend. "No; as I caught him, I wish to determine what to do with him, and I am bent upon having him for supper."

"But I say he shall be dried," said the first, again.

"I say he shall not !" cried the other.

"He shall !" yelled the first, poking his friend in the ribs.

"Do you mean to strike me ?" shouted the other, furiously, seizing a heavy club.

"Why not ?" roared his companion, in a great rage, catching hold of a young tree and brandishing it over his head.

Now the battle began. The little tailor was dropped and forgotten, while the giants used their clubs against each other with such a force that every stroke sounded as if one of the largest trees were felled to the ground. The great warrior who slew seven with one stroke would have run away, but became so frightened that he was utterly unable to move; so with closed eyes and shaking limbs he awaited the end of the struggle, thinking how foolish it was for him to leave his needle and thread for such exploits as killing dragons, serpents, and giants.

At length all was still, and the tailor ventured to open his eyes. Both giants were lying on the ground. Having knocked the clubs to pieces upon each other, they had torn trees from the ground and fought with them, until branches and stems lay scattered on all sides.

The little man walked around them a couple of times to see if they were really dead. He touched them with his foot, and at length he ventured to pluck the one by his long beard. Then he pulled out his sword and thrust it into the breast of the dead giant. When the other one had received the same treatment, the tailor sat down in the shade, wiped his forehead, and ate the rest of his bread-and-butter. He now returned to the palace and told the king that he had killed both giants. The entire court was greatly surprised, but the king said, " He has deserved the hundred gold pieces, and he shall have them."

"We all clearly see," observed a stout little general, "that a great and heroic spirit can dwell in a small body."

They went into the forest and found the dead monsters. "Look," exclaimed one of the courtiers, "how they have torn trees from the ground in the fearful struggle !"

"Wonderful, wonderful !" cried every one, looking admiringly at the little tailor, who drew himself up and looked proudly around.

"I should think," at length remarked one of the king's men, "that this brave man might also slay the unicorn which works havoc beyond the river "

"HE SWOONED AWAY"

"To be sure!" exclaimed the king. "Do you dare to engage in contest with the unicorn?" continued he, turning to the tailor. "I will give you two hundred gold pieces if you can manage to kill it!"

Now the tailor's dreams again awoke within him, and at this moment he did not remember that he had not really killed the giants. With sparkling eyes he turned to the king, exclaiming: "Your majesty, I shall kill the unicorn!"

The next day he was followed to the river by the whole court. The ferryman took him across the water, where he soon found himself in a forest, dense, wild, and desolate. No sooner was he left alone than the thought entered his head to turn back and run away from the danger, but in the same moment the unicorn burst through the bushes and came down upon him with glowing eyes, galloping wildly, and with the fearful frontal horn pointing to the very place where the tailor knew his heart was. There was no time even to think, and when the animal had come within four inches of him he swooned away and fell to the ground motionless. The monster, which came along at a furious rate, was, however, unable to stop. Like a fierce wind it passed him and ran its horn into the trunk of a large oak-tree with such a force that it was impossible to draw it back again. The tailor suffered no injury whatever. When he awoke from his swoon and found himself alive, the monster stood near him, kicking up the dust and leaves with its

hoofs, and howling with pain and fury. He saw
that his life was yet at stake, for i. the unicorn
succeeded in getting away no doubt it would again
turn upon him. So, however hard it went with him,
he must pull out his hacked sword, which he ran
into the neck of the unicorn with all his might.
A stream of green and black blood burst out
through the wound, while the animal began howling like all the swine in the land of Franconia taken
together. This was again too much for the heroic
tailor; he fainted, but when he awoke the animal
lay dead by his side. Without stopping to examine
it he repaired to the palace with the news of his
great deed. The whole city rejoiced over it. He
was led through the streets in triumph, and all the
church-bells rang for him. A gold chain was placed
around his neck by the king himself; two hundred
shining gold pieces were paid him; the queen kissed
his forehead, and all the great and small poets made
verse in honor of his heroism.

But our friend had had enough of both fright and
honor. He wished himself far from Franconia and
all its giants and unicorns. When he went to bed
in the evening he swore that nothing would induce
him to fight more of these frightful monsters, or to
dream of great deeds, for he had found that dreams
were dreams, and sometimes far from reality.

The next morning he packed his knapsack, stuffing the belt and money together at the bottom,
whereupon he went over to bid good-bye to the king

and the queen. The king did not wish, however, to part so soon from the great hero. "There is one more deed which you must accomplish before leaving us," he said. The tailor begged to be excused, but the king of Franconia possessed one remarkable quality : when he had taken something into his head he was bent upon having his will in spite of everything.

"What does your majesty ask me to do?" at length asked the tailor.

"I desire to have you kill a wild boar which haunts the woodlands on the borders of my domain," said the king. "If you succeed in killing this monster, three hundred gold pieces will be yours, and I promise to give you a duke's rank."

When the little man heard of the borders of the land he felt relieved, and thought : "If I can only manage to cross the frontiers, I care little about the boar, the money, and the duke's title, but will return home as fast as possible." He answered, however : "Your majesty's wish shall be fulfilled ; I will take the boar's life."

But his face lengthened a great deal when the king told him that one hundred brave knights were ready to follow him to the place, and that he himself intended to go also. "I am not the least afraid," concluded he, "when I am near your strong arm !"

Although the tailor did not at all enjoy the thought of having the king and the knights watch the fight between him and the boar, he made no objection, and so they started on their journey. The road was covered in many places with fragments of arms and legs from the poor victims of the raging beast.

"Your majesty," at length said one of the knights, "must not be exposed to the danger of meeting the boar. I propose that we stop here, and let this brave man face the monster alone. He will easily kill it."

"I agree with this friend of mine," observed the tailor at once.

The king assented, bidding his men to halt, while the hero pursued his way alone. So long as he could yet be seen by the king and his men he stepped briskly forward; but as soon as the trees concealed him from their view he uncovered his feet and walked along cautiously. Having thus pursued his way for a couple of hours, and thinking himself already out of danger, he noticed a little chapel among the trees, and thought that here he might pass the night undisturbed, when at once a fearful creaking was heard, and the boar came rushing against him as rapidly as the wind. It was immensely large, with a pair of gleaming, wicked eyes, and tusks of enormous length and size.

With a scream of terror the tailor made for the chapel, reached it, and jumped from one pew to another. the boar following him closely. At length he felt the animal's hot and fiery breath on the

"THE TAILOR MADE FOR THE CHAPEL"

back of his neck, when he saw an open window in front of him. Gathering all his force in a final jump, he skipped through the window and hastened, as soon as he had reached the ground, back to the entrance, the door of which he closed and bolted.

When he had thus escaped the animal and locked it up safely, he returned to the king and the knights, who greeted him with merry shouts.

"The animal was too small and unimportant for me to fight," said he. "I grasped it by the neck and threw it into the chapel. Now you may amuse yourselves by hunting and killing it. I only desire to receive the three hundred gold pieces, and to be allowed to return home."

His wish was granted at once, and with many thanks and blessings the King of Franconia parted with the great hero.

Tne tailor reached his native village safe and sound. One evening he was standing outside of his house, thinking how glad his wife would be to see him again, when he heard her voice within, crying for mercy, while a gruff answer followed, and a sound as if some one was beating her. The tailor's heroism at once awoke; he pushed the door open, seized his sword, and rushed into the room, where he found Mads, his wealthy neighbor, standing before the little woman, threatening to beat her with a thick cane. "He will never return home to you!" shouted Mads. "I will beat you until you give up every thought of him and consent to marry me."

"Yes, he will!" cried the little tailor; "and here he is, a great and honored man! With this sword I have killed two giants, a unicorn, and a wild boar, and six hundred gold pieces were my reward." He looked fiercely at Mads, and continued: "I ought to kill you for beating my wife, you wretch; but I feel too great for such trifling deeds. Out with you!" shouted he, pulling forth the rusty sword and pointing to the open door. "Out with you! Do you hear?"

Mads retreated through the door in great haste, but the tailor and his little wife clasped each other in their arms He told her how he had accomplished these great deeds, but that he was tired of leading such a hard life as a hero must necessarily lead. Therefore he had returned home.

The little tailor became a wealthy man; he had his own carriage and horses, and henceforth he sewed only tor his own pleasure. The blacksmith, his devoted friend, received a liberal share of these riches which were obtained by manful deeds, and so well deserved.

A WELL-DRESSED Jutlander once took a drop too much, and consequently lost command of his legs, landing at full length in the middle of the high-road, where he fell asleep. While he was lying in this state another wayfarer passed him. When he observed the Jutlander's fine stockings and compared them with his own, which were old and worn, he saw his chance to draw the good stockings off the Jutlander's feet and to replace them with his own. Upon doing this, he walked on.

When the Jutlander had slept until he was somewhat more sober, a man came driving along, shouting: "Keep your legs by yourself or I shall run over them!" The Jutlander awoke, lifted his head, and looked at the legs; but when he noticed a pair of gray, ragged stockings, and remembered that his own were pretty, white, and brand-new, he lay quietly down again, answering: "Drive on! These are not my legs!"

NCE upon a time there lived a king in a country far away from ours. He had three sons, any of whom he could select as his successor. As he was a very old man, all his counsellors and friends among the noblemen besought him to determine which of the three princes he would choose.

The king promised to make the decision in a month's time, and at the end of the first week he requested his oldest son to be ready to ride out with him the following morning at a certain early hour.

Early in the morning, yet later than they had agreed, the prince appeared in the king's rooms. His father said that he desired to dress, and asked the young man to fetch his garments. The prince turned to a valet, and bid him bring them. The valet inquired, however, which ones he should bring, whereupon the young man repeated the question to the king. He replied, "My overcoat." "Which one?" then asked the valet. So the king was obliged to make yet another explanation about this matter; and thus they went on, until at length he was dressed to his satisfaction.

He now told his son to saddle his horse and bring it forward. The young man willingly complied, ordering the Royal groom to make his father's horse ready for a ride. "Which one of them?" inquired the groom, and the prince was again obliged to seek information from the king. Thus it went on, until at length the horse was standing in front of the door ready for the king to mount. Now the king declared that he could not go, and asked the prince to do so, and to notice carefully all that he saw on his way, in order that he might be prepared on his return to relate all that was important and noteworthy.

So the prince mounted, and rode, accompanied by all the knights and noblemen, through the city. They formed a stately parade, which was headed by a choice corps of kettle-drummers, trumpeters, and flautists. When they returned to the palace, the king asked his son what he had seen and how he had liked it. "Well enough," replied the young man, "but the kettle-drummers made too much noise!"

At the end of another week the king called his second-oldest son, and repeated to him the same instructions as were given in the case of his brother. This young man acted exactly like the other prince.

A few days later the king bid his youngest son appear before him the following morning by daybreak. He came in due time, and finding his father yet sleeping, waited for him to awake. When this took place he entered the sleeping-room, bowed reverently to the monarch, and received orders to fetch his clothes. He inquired very carefully as to the king's wishes, allowed no one but himself to bring the articles, and assisted him in putting them on, declaring that no one but he himself should help his father. At length the king was dressed to his satisfaction, whereupon he requested the young man to order the horse ready for a ride. Having inquired about his father's wishes regarding the saddle, bridle, spurs, sword, and the rest of the equipment, he went into the stable and arranged it all according to the directions which he had received. When all was ready the king had determined, however, to remain at home, but asked the prince to ride out into the city and give careful attention to all that he heard and saw.

Mounting the horse, the prince first proceeded to the centre of the city, where he inspected the Royal treasury and the churches. Then he proceeded to examine the fortifications around the city, mustered the army, held exercises with the soldiers, and took a general view of the condition of things.

Towards evening he returned home, and when the king asked him to relate what he had seen, he hesitated, saying that he was afraid of arousing his anger. But when the king bid him speak freely, the prince stated that although he (the king) was a skilful man and an able ruler, he did not seem as clever as he might be, otherwise he would have conquered the whole world long ago. His army was so large and well equipped that this would be an easy matter for him!

This reproach pleased the king so much that on the appointed day when the council was to listen to his decision in the matter of the succession, he announced that his youngest son would be best fitted for governing the land. Although his two older sons were good and able young men in their way, he would choose neither of them, as they had both fallen short of his expectations.

NCE on a time there was a king who advertised in the papers that if any one proved able to make his daughter say, "That is a lie!" he would be at liberty to marry her.

Although this sounds strange, it is as true as all the other stories I have told. It might be objected that kings do not advertise in the papers, but I who know so many of them say that such is, indeed, often the case, and there is no reason to doubt my words. Newspapers receive advertisements from any one who can pay for them, from the king and downward, or from the beggar and upward; and the king of whom we are now speaking paid a great sum, moreover, for having his law — kings' words are always law—inserted in the papers.

It might also be objected that a princess would not use such language as I mentioned.

They might! They do, indeed, sometimes! I have heard many princesses say words much worse than these, and yet they were fine girls, whom all liked. It matters little what you say, but it matters a great deal what you are!

So this princess, who was as brave and good as any girl living, was to be married to the man who could make her say the words: "That is a lie!"

There were many who thought it would be an easy matter to tell a lie to the princess, for the world always has more of this sort of thing than is needed. But she was so sweet and good, and trusted people so well, that it was a very difficult matter to tell her anything that she did not believe at all. One after another the suitors came with great hopes and went away disappointed.

In a little house near the borders of the same land there lived a man whose only son was known far and wide on account of his great foolishness. When this young man heard the news of the king's announcement, he put on his wooden shoes and his cap, said good-bye to his parents, and went straight to the palace, where he found the princess. When she learned his errand she proposed their taking a walk together, whereupon they strolled into the court-yard and through the gardens. Here the boy—Claus was his name—stopped and said:

"What immense cabbage you have here!"

"It might be smaller," returned the princess.

"Well," resumed Claus, "after all, it is nothing to my father's cabbage. Once we were building a new barn, and sixteen carpenters were working on the building; a shower came up, and all sixteen men took shelter under one of the leaves. After a while one of them thrust his knife through it, to see if the rain was over ; but so much water had been collected on the surface that it poured down immediately in such quantities that every carpenter was drowned."

"That cabbage must have been large, indeed!" remarked the princess.

The young man was, however, not so easily disposed of. "You have a good-sized barn," remarked he, "and well built, too."

"Yes," replied the princess, "but my father is the king, you know, and so it could not be smaller."

"True enough," continued Claus, "but *our* barn is so immense that while a cow walks through it from one end to the other she may become old and worn out."

"A large barn, indeed !" observed the young lady.

Claus appeared unaffected. "Your sheep," he pursued, "seem to be large and well kept, but my father's sheep are larger yet. Their tails are so heavy that we are obliged to tie them to big wagons, and when we want some meat for a soup, all that we need is to go and cut off a piece of one of these tails. Then we have enough for several hundred persons. When they are sheared, we hire sixteen wood-cutters to cut off the wool with their axes. Each animal keeps them working for eight days."

"Fine sheep they must be, I am sure!" remarked the princess.

But Claus could not think of giving up yet.

"Your chickens are very good-looking, too," said he; "but ours are still better. Their feathers are so long and stiff that they can be used for ships' masts, and their eggs are so large that when we saw them through in the middle we have two good boats. The hens lay so many eggs that we send away ten wagon-loads of them every day. My father loads them, and I drive to town with them. Some days ago we were a little careless, for our load became so high that before I realized anything I was standing at the moon. While I looked around, the load was upset, and there I stood, unable to return. I found some cobweb, however, fastened one end to a tree, and lowered myself downward. The cobweb did not reach far enough, and I was obliged to jump, which I did. I landed in a church, where the congregation was just taking up a collection for the poor. Your father was there; he sat in the middle of the floor, with an old nightcap on his head, and it was drawn down over his ears. His pockets were filled with silver and gold, but he was so covetous that when his turn came he gave only two paltry copper pennies to the poor. His nose was—"

"That is a lie, if you wish to know it!" interrupted the princess, turning scarlet with anger. "My father never wears a nightcap in the church, and he is not covetous!"

"Quite possible," replied the young man, "but that does not matter, for I have made you utter what you never said before, and so you are mine and I am yours!"

The princess could not deny it, and they were married ; but since that time she has never caught Claus telling lies. Therefore they live happily together.

THE OBSTINATE SHOEMAKER

NCE upon a time there was a shoemaker who doted on pancakes. One day he asked his wife to bake him some for dinner. She replied that she was will-ing enough, but there was no pan in the house, and if he wished for pancakes, he had better go and borrow one from the neighbor. He complied, and at dinner he ate as rapidly as his wife could bake. When they had finished their meal, the shoe-maker told his wife to carry the pan back to its owner. She refused, however, and declared that she did not like to carry back borrowed articles. As he insisted, they nearly came to blows, but finally they agreed to go to work, and the one who spoke first should return the pan to its owner.

The shoemaker seated himself on his platform, sewing and handling his shoes and his leather. His wife took her seat by her spinning-wheel, and soon they were working as if life depended upon their handiness. Neither uttered a sound.

In a short time a squire who lived in the neigh-borhood, and who had given a pair of shoes to the shoemaker to repair, passed the house, bid his coachman stop, and sent his servant in, asking him to see whether his shoes were finished.

The servant walked in, greeted, and delivered his errand.

"Whew, whe-ew, whe-e-e-e-e-ew!" whistled the shoemaker, who sat on his three-legged chair, battling with the air, and sewing diligently. As the servant could not draw a single word from him by way of answer, he turned to the woman, whose spinning-wheel went so rapidly that sparks flew from it. "How is it," asked he. "that your husband does not answer when I talk to him?" "Tralala-lide-lide-raderade lidelidelidelidelide ralala!" sang the woman at the top of her voice, spinning with all her might and looking straight into his face. The servant saw that there was nothing for him to do but return to his master in the carriage. The two people must have lost their senses!

When he reached the carriage, the squire asked him if the shoes were finished.

"I don't know," replied he; "the shoemaker and his wife must have lost their senses. The man whistles and the woman sings, and those are all the sounds they utter. They would not say as much as one plain word."

The squire alighted to see what had happened to the persons within. "If they pretend to make fun of their customers, I shall teach them manners," said he to himself. "Here they are, and here I come." So he opened the door and walked in.

The shoemaker whistled with all his might as soon as the squire opened his mouth to speak. The woman sang and shouted with all her might; but neither of them seemed to notice his question as to the shoes. At length he became vexed, seized his riding-whip, and lifted it over the woman's shoulders. The shoemaker stole a glance at them, but said nothing.

A minute later the whip was dancing lustily across the shoulder - blades of the woman, who at once struck up a new tune, but less merry than before. But this was too much for the shoemaker. He jumped from his seat, rushed at the squire, and bid him stop.

"Ah," exclaimed the squire, "you are not mute. I am pleased to know that your voice is in as good working order as your fingers seem to be."

"You spoke first," cried the woman to her husband, "and you must carry the pan back to our neighbor!"

Now they told the squire of their quarrel and agreement, and it greatly amused him when he learned that he had settled the dispute. I do not know whether or not his shoes were finished; but that cuts no figure. I saw, however, the shoemaker when he slouched through the back yard with the pan carefully concealed under his coat. It served him right that his wife won the wager. What do *you* think?

THE MERCHANT

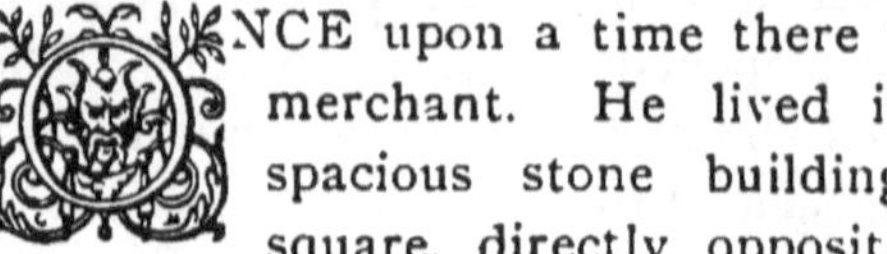NCE upon a time there was a wealthy merchant. He lived in a beautiful, spacious stone building, in a large square, directly opposite a cathedral. The front was adorned with monuments of great value. A high staircase, which led from the street to the entrance, was furnished with a magnificent iron railing of excellent workmanship, with gilded balls and ornaments. The owner of this exquisite mansion was immensely rich. He imported in his own ships, from countries far away, choice fruit and wine, ivory, and fragrant spices. The floor in his large hall consisted of gold coin placed on edge, and when he invited his friends to pass an evening at his home, all the dishes were served on gold plates. Every cup and plate, every knife and fork in his house was made of pure gold. There seemed to be no end to his wealth.

At length the merchant died, leaving his whole property to his only son, the handsomest young man in the whole town, of excellent character, and always contented and glad. He had a smile and a pleasant word for every one, so in his short life he had found more friends than the old merchant had ever had, in spite of his seventy years. When the young man succeeded his father as master of the magnificent house, a great many of his friends took up their abode with him. They ate at his table, drank of his wine, and stayed with him days and nights, praising his great kindness and generosity, his open hand, and his open heart. Whenever they were in need of money and mentioned it to him, he pointed to an old chest in a corner, saying, "Take what you need, and return it when you can." At length his friends made themselves so much at home that they found their way into the chest without asking permission, so in a little while the old book-keeper, who had served the house for nearly forty years, told his young master that all the money was gone.

"Well, the chest must be filled again," said the young man, carelessly. "There is the floor in the great hall! Break it up, and fill the chest. We can have a marble floor laid in its place."

His orders were obeyed, and there seemed to be money enough to fill the chest for all time to come. Every one thought that the marble floor looked much handsomer than the golden one; besides, it was not as expensive, and the friends did not know how to praise enough the wisdom and foresight of their friend. A great many poor persons who heard of his generosity came and asked to be helped from time to time, and their wishes were at once granted.

The young merchant was to be married to a very beautiful young lady, the daughter of a wise counsellor. When the time came for their wedding the groom wished to give his bride a golden carriage and six milk-white horses; but the old book-keeper shook his head, and said that they could already see the bottom of the chest, and there were no more floors from which it could be again filled. On hearing this the young man called his friends together, and said to them that as he was in need of money he was obliged to ask them help him. Now the time had come when he needed some of the money which they had borrowed from him at different times. None of them was willing to comply, however: had he loaned them money, he had also told them that they might pay him whenever they could spare it. He had lived like a fool; he had been very reckless; he never cut his coat according to his cloth. To give money to the poor was the same as robbing one's friends! Their friendship was at an end, and they would be ashamed even to be seen with him in the streets hereafter.

Disappointed and angry with these men for whom he had done so much, the young merchant went to the home of his betrothed, thinking that she might at least give him some consolation. His friends had already been there, however, and talked to the girl's parents in such a manner that the young man was

"NONE OF THEM WAS WILLING TO COMPLY"

not allowed even to see her. She was locked up in a room, where she sat moping and nearly crying her eyes out. It went no better with the young man at other places : all those to whom he turned for help shook their heads or abused him like a pick-pocket, but no one raised a finger to help him.

At length he returned home, utterly depressed and despondent ; but the old book-keeper told him to pick up courage. Some of their customers abroad owed them large sums of money. "I have saved a little from time to time," said he ; "this will enable me to keep up the business until we can be helped. Here is a list of those whom we may expect to pay their debts. I advise you to go and see them. There is money enough here to pay your fare."

The merchant embraced the true old man, and thanked him for his great faithfulness and devotion. Having received much good advice from his old friend, he set out on his journey.

It seemed, however, that misfortune had determined to follow him, for all who could pay their debts refused to do so, while the rest were willing enough, but had no money. At length the young man had nothing to do but return home.

One day, towards evening, he reached an inn. A storm had overtaken him, and an icy-cold drizzle made him shiver from head to foot. He had been obliged to sell his horse and discharge his servant, and a few pennies were all that he had left in his purse, although home was still far away. Tired and famished, he knocked at the door, and his voice was neither cheerful nor courageous when he asked for food and shelter.

The stout host with his shining face looked at the young traveller's well-worn dress and his faded hat, whereupon he said, gruffly and unkindly : "All the rooms are occupied, and all that we can give you is a place at the supper-table if you can pay for it. Beggars and landlopers we have no use for here."

The young merchant asked if he could not be allowed to sleep in the hay-loft. It was a stormy evening, and he was tired out.

"No," replied his host; "people who have no money are not *my* people. I don't care what becomes of them."

"Why can't you," said one of the guests, who was sitting in a corner with several others before a steaming bowl of punch, "let this young man sleep in the old ruin across the way?"

"In the ruin!" repeated the host, grinning slyly. "Why not? That will be a splendid place to rest," continued he, turning to the young man, "if you are not afraid of ghosts."

The merchant's pride awoke. "I am afraid of no person, living or dead," said he, looking straight at the landlord's cunning features.

"Come along, then," exclaimed the man, "and I will show you the place." He led the way out of the inn and up an avenue of old chestnut-trees into a dejected ruin, where time had left only a few rooms free from destruction. Into one of these they went. It was a large, gloomy room, with a few pieces of furniture : an old bed, with stiff, faded curtains, a solid oak table, two easy-chairs, and an old iron-clad chest.

Soon a fire was made in the half-crumbled fire-place, whereupon the landlord bid the young man good-night, promising to send him some supper. In a little while two servant-girls appeared with lighted candles, which were placed on the table, and a basket, from which they produced a piece of ham, bread-and-butter, and a chicken. Upon this the girls returned to the inn, while the young man hung up his wet mantle near the fireplace and sat down to satisfy his hunger. As soon as he had eaten, he went to bed and slept soundly.

In a few hours he awoke. Everything was quiet; the fire burned slowly, and no sound was heard. Glancing towards the window to see if it was night or morning, the merchant caught sight of the tall, stout figure of a man standing in front of the table. He wore a black suit, pointed shoes, and over his shoulders was hanging a red mantle, held together in front by an old-fashioned silver buckle.

The young man felt his blood run cold, and his hair began to stand on end; but in the next minute he was possessed by some of his old courage, which had been strengthened by the warm room and the good supper. He sat up in bed, glancing at the stern features of his unknown visitor, until the latter approached one of the old-fashioned, high-backed easy-chairs, and pointed to its seat with an imperious gesture. As the occupant of the bed made no effort to move, the ghost again pointed to the chair, while his features became threatening. The merchant, who had now entirely governed his fears, threw the pillows aside and jumped into the room, where he walked up to the chair and seated himself.

The ghost immediately opened his mantle and produced a glass filled with white foam, which he placed on the table, laying a shining razor beside it. The young man in the chair now began to shiver all over his body, and thought that his last moments had come. He closed his eyes and remained sitting immovable, when suddenly he felt something moist and cold on his face and head. He now realized that the ghost was not intending to kill him, but only to shave his head and chin. So it was; in a little while his head was as even and shining as an ivory ball. The man laid down his razor on the table, looked imploringly at the merchant, and passed his fingers across his own head and chin. Our friend thought this quite amusing. No doubt the ghost wished to be shaved also, and a few minutes later the operation was performed. Then the ghost opened his mouth for the first time, and said: "Thanks, my young friend! You have saved me, and now I can sleep peacefully."

"To say the truth," replied the merchant, "I have

the same desire. You awoke me at an untimely hour! But why could you not rest peacefully before?"

"I lived a foolish, heedless life," replied the ghost. "I had enough of gold and silver, all that I wished for, and even more, but I squandered my wealth on those whom I called my friends, and they helped me faithfully to spend it, until one day I suddenly died. When I arrived at the gate of heaven, Saint Peter told me that I was doomed to walk about at night until I found some one who would permit me to shave him, and who would do me the same service."

"When you are wealthy," observed the young man, "you can always count on a great number of friends. I had many until I lost my wealth."

"Yes," replied the ghost, "I know them all."

"You know them?" cried the merchant, startled by this intelligence.

"Yes; but ask no questions. Put on your clothes and follow me!"

The young man complied, whereupon the ghost seized one of the candlesticks and conducted him into the cellar, where they stopped before a very old iron chest. "This," said the owner of the red mantle, "is yours. Until I was dead I did not know that it existed, but if I had found it before, no doubt its contents would have vanished with the rest of my wealth. This chest is filled with gold coin. When you leave this dismal ruin, which was once a beautiful mansion, take it away with you, and use the money with care and caution."

When they returned to the room above, the merchant said : "I do not understand why you were doomed to such work as shaving people."

"Do you not understand," replied the ghost, "that I had been shaved by all my friends, and that I was now obliged to do the same? That was my penalty for living a life without aim and goal ; but now I am free."

The young man mused for a moment, and said : "But was the money not all your own? Did you not have a right to use it as you pleased?"

The ghost answered, gravely : "No, it was not. I held it in trust, as every wealthy man does. The day will come when we shall account for all that we have said and done, and for the manner in which we spent the money which God intrusted to our care !"

Every word fell heavily upon the mind of the young man. He plunged into a deep revery, from which he did not awake until the daylight had found its way through the green, narrow windows. Lifting his head, he noticed that the landlord stood in the open door, gazing at him with a wicked expression of joy in his small, deep set eyes.

"I see that the man with the red mantle has paid you a visit," said he, blinking maliciously at his guest.

"Yes," replied the merchant, "and he proved to be an excellent man. We talked a great deal of people whom we both know, and of you, too."

"THE GHOST CONDUCTED HIM INTO THE CELLAR"

"Of me?" cried the landlord.

"Yes. The ghost promised to visit you in a few days and shave your head and chin. He said that he had kept his eye on you for a great length of time."

"Gracious!" shouted he. "How can I escape him? I would die of fear if I ever awoke and found him in my room."

"I shall tell him to-night," answered the young man, "that you would prefer not to be shaved as I was. But in return you must keep me here for a month, and when I am ready to return home I wish to borrow your horses and carriage."

The landlord promised this, and implored him to do all that was in his power to prevent his being shaved by the terrible ghost, of which he had heard so many fearful tales.

In the course of the next four weeks the young merchant's hair had again grown into its usual length, so he left the ruin in the landlord's carriage, and returned home with the chest, which was found to contain an immense sum of money. The old book-keeper initiated him into the duties of the business, which grew rapidly, and brought him back his old wealth in the course of a short time.

As soon as it was known that the merchant had returned home with immense riches, his friends again presented themselves at his door. The young man hired, however, a couple of stout stone-cutters, and as soon as the friends appeared they were thrown into the street more rapidly than they could realize, and never dared to call a second time.

But the young man hastened to the house of his sweetheart, and told her parents all that had happened. The girl had remained faithful to him, and there was now no objection to their marriage. There was no golden carriage ; but they were contented with less.

This is the story of the merchant who learned to be faithful to his trust.

NCE upon a time there were two villages lying a few miles from each other, in a certain part of the country. Their names were Plaintown and Hilltown.

In our day the people of Plaintown are considered about as clever as the rest of their countrymen, but in olden times they were different. Their fertile soil and abundance of crops, their fragrant hop-gardens and extensive farms, filled their chests and drawers with gold and silver. Of hills and woods they had no idea, and any one knows that he who has never needed to climb a hill or remove the trees which stand in his way is liable to become idle and lazy, and to be less efficient than others who learn to face and overthrow the difficulties which are in their way.

Hilltown had hills and woods. The soil was ot very rich, and produced only moderate crops, so those who cultivated it were forced to work hard for the necessities of life. But they learned more by working so hard than their friends in Plaintown who lived at ease.

In Hilltown there was a man called Eric. One day he had the good fortune to catch a fox which had long disturbed the peace in his poultry-yard. He determined not to kill the animal, but tied a rope around Reynard's neck and determined to sell him to any one who might buy him. As he went along a by-road, a man from Plaintown came driving along in great state. His name was Christopher. When he caught sight of the fox he stopped his horses, shouting: "What sort of creature is that, hey? I never saw its like before."

Eric from Hilltown stopped and looked at the stranger and his two beautiful mares. As soon as he found out that the man could have come from no other place than Plaintown, he replied: "It is a sheep-painter."

"A sheep-painter!" shouted the Plaintowner. "What use do you make of him?"

"He paints my sheep red," returned Eric.

"Is it possible, indeed?" said Christopher.

"The greatest truth you ever heard," asserted the other. "If you let him paint the wool, you never need to have it dyed afterwards."

"A great deal of money might be saved in that ma er," observed Christopher again.

"Depend upon it, my friend!" said Eric. "He is expensive. Yes, yes, he is *very* expensive, but you save the cost of dyeing, you know, in the future. *This* expense comes only once."

"Of course—of course!" rejoined Christopher.

"'IT IS A SHEEP-PAINTER'"

"That is true. How—how much will you take for him?"

"I did not think of selling him," said Eric, "but I will do you a favor if I can, so I v ll let him go for seventy dollars."

"That is a great deal,' remarked the man from Plaintown. "Three fine cows might be bought for that money."

"I know," answered Eric; "and you have a right to choose what will be most useful to you, of course." So he turned around and began to walk on.

"Wait—wait a moment!" shouted the rich man. "Why can't we talk about it? I will give you fifty."

"Take him, then," answered Eric, turning back, "and you are welcome to him."

The bargain was closed, and Reynard changed owner. "Just let me tell you," explained Eric, "how to treat him. When you want him to paint some of your sheep, put him into the fold and keep the door well closed for two weeks. He finds his own food, so you need not disturb him at all until he tells you that the work is done."

When Christopher returned home with his sheep-painter, it was determined to put him to work at once. He was led into the fold, and the door was carefully closed in order to prevent any one from disturbing him.

In a week Christopher's wife became curious to see how far the work had progressed. She peeped through the door and said that she could see a great many red spots. So they concluded that the painter was at work, and determined to leave him alone another week, that he might finish his task.

When the two weeks had passed, the Plainfielder and his wife opened the door of the sheepfold and walked in. Both sheep-painter and sheep were gone. A few bloody hides and bones alone remained. A hole in the wall showed the way in which the painter had escaped.

"I have been cheated — shamefully deceived!" cried Christopher, while his wife began to cry and lament over the sheep. "But I will take revenge. Such a long, shrivelled rascal! I shall paint him, indeed, until he is both red and blue!" He made his horses and carriage ready, selected his best whip, and set out to cool his rage upon the cunning man in Hilltown who had treated him so shamefully.

Eric at once guessed his errand when he saw Christopher approaching, and running into the kitchen, he seized a pot with boiling soup and placed it on a stone in the yard. As the boiling did not cease at once, the first thing which Christopher caught sight of when he drove into the yard was this pot, which seemed to boil without fire or spark, standing on the cold stone. He at once forgot the sheep-painter and his own thoughts of revenge. Such a pot must be a great marvel. Before he drove out of the yard again he had bought it for fifty dollars. This time he felt sure the cunning Hilltown man could not deceive him, for

"SUCH A POT MUST BE A GREAT MARVEL"

he had seen himself how the pot boiled with all its might, without fire, on the cold stone.

As soon as he was home again he determined to try the pot. It was filled with water and placed on a stone in the yard, and the whole family stood around it, watching to see it boil, and gazing with all their might at this wonderful article.

"You had better tell it to start," said the woman to her husband, after a while.

"You had better begin to boil," said Christopher to the pot.

They waited one hour, and another, but not even the faintest smoke could be seen.

"It is time to start!" shouted Christopher to the pot, but it did not heed him at all, and at length they were convinced that they had again been hood-winked by the deceitful man in Hilltown.

Christopher swore that this time his man should not escape him. With six other Plainfielders he set out to work a fearful revenge upon the sly man in Hilltown, who did not seem to possess as much honor even as the sheep-painter.

The seven men arrived at Hilltown, and every one saw that they were fearfully excited. When they arrived at Eric's farm, all alighted and entered the dwelling-house.

"How do you do?" said Christopher to the culprit's wife, who was alone in the room. "Where is your rascal of a husband?"

"Eric is in the woods," returned the woman.

"The aldermen are holding a meeting, and you may go and see him there."

"How do we find him?" inquired one of the men.

"When you reach the gate which opens from the road into the forest, you will see a large elm to the right," replied she. "All that you need do is to knock a dozen times on the tree with your large clubs, then Eric will come out and talk with you. Be sure of that!"

The seven Plainfielders followed her directions to the letter. When they reached the large elm they stopped and listened. Quite right; there was a buzzing within the tree like at an alderman's meeting, where the wise fathers speak all at once. "Now he shall have what he has deserved," said the seven men to one another, fetching the tree some hard blows with their clubs. But the wasps within the old and rotten trunk took this action much amiss. They at once fell upon the seven intruders with such good will and such effect that all took to their heels, having tried in vain to make front against the enemy.

They returned to the carriage as rapidly as their legs would carry them, and drove out of Hilltown with swelled noses and pains in all their limbs. To render their rout complete, Eric had seated himself in a tall tree near a bridge built across a small creek, which the men must pass. As soon as the defeated Plainfielders arrived there, he began to sound an old trumpet with all his might. The horses immediately fell into a mad career, throwing the seven stout men out of the carriage in the middle of the bridge. They rolled over the edge and fell into the water, which cooled both their swollen faces and their rage They returned home richer in experience, but determined never to approach Hilltown again in all their lives, but to devise better plans for a revenge than those which had been so shamefully frustrated by their cunning enemy. I do not know how well their plans were carried out.

HERE was once a princess who possessed three wonderful gifts: Whenever she wept, pearls rolled out from the corners of her eyes; when she smiled, roses dropped from her cheeks ; and with every step she made barefooted, a gold piece was left in the dust under her heels. The king and the whole nation rejoiced over these wonders, for the treasury never became empty, and whenever there was any need of money, the girl was always ready to take a walk barefooted through the rooms of the Royal palace.

On such occasions a number of courtiers always followed her with large crystal bowls, gathering up the gold pieces left by her footsteps.

The fame of Princess Rosamund spread far and wide, and no sooner had it reached Prince Hermes, a son of the king of one of the adjoining countries, than he asked his father's permission to go and win her hand. The king consented ; but when every thing was ready for his son's departure, a war broke out, and the young prince was called away by other duties. While he fought gallantly against the ene-

ROSES, PEARLS, AND GOLD PIECES

mies, the queen's first lady of honor proposed to the Royal couple that the beautiful princess be invited to visit them, so that the brave prince would, on his return from the battle-fields, find her there already.

The king and queen at once determined to carry out this plan, so the lady of honor was selected as a worthy messenger for the delicate errand of proposing a union between the youngest members of the two renowned and illustrious families, and set out accordingly on her journey.

The lady of honor was, however, a witch, who had planned to deceive the royal family. She had a daughter whom she wished the prince to marry, but who was neither good nor pretty. When she arrived at her destination she told her errand, and showed Princess Rosamund the picture of Prince Hermes. The girl declared herself ready to give him her hand in marriage if he proved as noble and good as the picture seemed to indicate. Her parents readily gave their consent, whereupon everything was made ready for their daughter's departure. Before Rosamund took leave of her home, she walked three times around the large court-yard barefooted for the benefit of the poor, who were permitted to pick up the gold coin that she left behind her.

Rosamund and the lady of honor drove in a carriage by themselves, followed by an escort of stately noblemen and guards. When they had

travelled a long distance, the witch made a fearful
storm gather around them. It became as dark as
the darkest night around the place ; the escort
was scattered, and the daughter of the evil woman
emerged from the depths of a black cloud. She
and her mother seized Rosamund, who cried tor-
rents of pearls, and robbed her of her beautiful
eyes, which they threw into a ditch at one side of
the road, while the princess was herself pushed out
into the mud at the other side. Now the daughter of the witch seated herself in the carriage with
her mother, and away they drove to the home of
Prince Hermes.

The unfortunate princess was in the mean time
lying in the ditch, bewailing her cruel fate. At
length two wagoners who passed along the road
heard her voice, and pulled her out of the disagreeable place. Her shoes were lost, her stockings were
torn, and when she walked there was a sound like
the ring of gold from under her feet. As one of
the men bent down to find out the reason of this
sound he noticed the gold pieces.

The two men at once became mad with joy. They
forced the princess to walk about all the livelong
day, the one leading her by her hand while his comrade busied himself with gathering up the money.
Finally she fainted from sheer exhaustion and pain.
She was, in fact, more dead than alive, and her feet
bled from the many sharp stones that had hurt
them over and over again. The wagoners now

were afraid that they had killed her, so they left
her lying in the road and pursued their way as
rapidly as their horses would run.   In a little while
a gardener happened to pass the place where the
princess had been left.   Being a kind and charitable
man, he lifted the poor girl into his carriage and
took her to his home.   She was sick a very long
time, but finally she began to recover and regain
her health and strength.   One day she happened to
hear the gardener tell his wife of Prince Hermes's
and Princess Rosamund's marriage, the wedding
having just been celebrated with great pomp and
splendor.   People had assembled from all over the
country, said the gardener, to catch a glimpse of
the princess who left gold coin in her footprints and
shed roses by her smiles.   None of these wonders had
occurred, however ; the princess was not at all what
had been expected, and no one had proved able to
make her smile or weep.   She was sullen and disagreeable to all, even to the prince, her husband,
who did his best to make her happy, but without
the slightest effect.   She beat all her maids with a
broomstick, so at length no one could be induced
to serve her.

The gardener's wife said : " It seems to me that
the poor girl whom you found in the road looks so
gentle and good that she might serve the princess
and satisfy her.   If we could only find a pair of eyes
for her, it might be worth trying."

" There is a woman in town," answered her husband, "who trades in eyes. I will go and see whether she has a pair which may serve this girl."

The next morning the good man went out with a large basket filled with fine apples, which he brought to the old woman, asking her for a pair of eyes. She sat reading in a large book with big red letters, and merely reaching into a tub near her, she produced a pair of eyes, handed them to the gardener, and pointed to the door.

When the gardener reached home the balls were at once placed in the girl's head. But the effect was remarkable: she remained sitting at the same place all the day, and fixed her glance upon a small hole in the wall. When this had been going on for eight days the gardener brought the eyes back to the woman, complaining that they did not at all seem to fit the person who desired to use them, and asking for another pair in exchange.

"No wonder," said the woman. "These are cat's eyes, and the girl has most likely looked at the hole in the wall because she expected a mouse to appear. Here is another pair—beautiful blue eyes, which I found in a ditch a few days ago. Try them."

The girl tried them, and found them to be her own. Now the gardener followed her to the palace, where the princess at once engaged her service. Although Rosamund tried her best to please her, it was very difficult, and the poor girl suffered much from her sullen and whimsical mistress.

One day she was waiting on her when Prince

Hermes came into the room. Rosamund was so moved by seeing him that she dropped a silver coffee-pot which she was holding in her hands upon the white silk carpet. The princess arose furious, rushed at her, and began to box her ears. The tears started in Rosamund's eyes, and soon a stream of pearls rolled across the floor towards the place where Prince Hermes was standing.

" Pearls !" cried he. " Are your tears pearls?"

Rosamund wiped her eyes and smiled, but at the same moment two beautiful roses fell from her cheeks. The prince called his parents, and when they had heard of her sufferings he pulled out his sword and killed the witch and her daughter After-wards he married the right Rosamund, and then people were no longer deceived, for she smiled so often and so willingly at every one that the whole land was happy. I saw her yesterday, and she smiled at me too, and one of the roses stands before me in a glass of water.

HERE was once a soldier who had served his country faithfully for eight years, and staked his life many times both on land and water, both in war and in peace. At the end of the eight years he was to receive wages for his faithful service. But the war had caused the king so much expense that at the time when the soldier asked for his pay there remained only a few copper pennies in the treasury.

"Now, my friend," said the king—mark, he called the soldier his friend!—"you see how it is. There is nothing in the treasury."

"There is a little left, your majesty," answered the soldier, "give me three pennies, that is enough!"

"Take them," returned the king; "then I have five left, and those I will save. We may need them some day."

"Yes, indeed," observed the soldier, "and good-bye to your majesty."

"Good-bye, and take good care of yourself," cried the king; "if I can ever do anything for you, let me know of it!"

"SO HE GAVE THE OLD WOMAN ONE OF HIS PENNIES"

"Much obliged!" answered the soldier, "and farewell."

When he had walked on a distance he met an old woman who asked him for a penny. "A penny!" exclaimed he. "Three pennies are all I have, but it makes no difference whether there are three or two." So he gave the old woman one of his pennies, and walked on. In a little while he met another old woman who begged for a penny. "Whether I have two or one is all the same," said he, and immediately handed her one. Soon afterwards a third woman stopped and asked him for a little help. "One penny 's my whole property," replied the soldier, "besides an old shirt and a pair of stockings without heels; but one or none it is all the same, so here is the penny. You are welcome to keep it."

The three old women were, however, one and the same, and this one was, moreover, a great and good fairy who had only assumed the shape of an old, wrinkled woman in order to try the soldier, whose free and generous ways she liked. If his heart was as good and brave as she thought, he deserved to be rewarded. So she told him all, and added that he might make three wishes, which would all be fulfilled.

The soldier was much surprised, and at first did not know what to wish for. But at length he said, "I wish to have and hold the grace and good-will of God."

"That is a good wish," replied the fairy, " and so far as I can help you, you shall have it !"

" I further wish," continued he, "that my knapsack may never be worn out, and that all I wish to be placed in it may remain there until I desire to have it out again."

"It is all granted you," returned the fairy, smilingly ; "and now I bid you good-bye in good earnest." So they separated, and the soldier pursued his way homeward. As he walked along he could not help stopping from time to time to think how strange it was that he could wish anything into his knapsack.

Towards evening he arrived at a castle, and as he was very hungry he went in and asked the cook for some supper. "I would gladly give you what you ask for," answered she, "but the master of this castle is so covetous that he locks up the pantry, and allows none ot us to eat or take more than he gives us." So the soldier was obliged to walk away without even a drink of water. He promised himself, however, to remember the covetous squire.

The next morning he reached a small farm where he knew that his sweetheart was living. The buildings looked neglected and decayed, but the soldier walked briskly in, and found everything as of old, except for the great poverty which was everywhere apparent. The farm belonged to the wealthy squire, and he was not the man to allow any of his tenants to be very comfortable.

"What ails you?" asked the soldier, seeing that both his sweetheart and her mother looked careworn and sorrowful. They told him how the wealthy man defrauded them on all occasions, so that they could hardly gain their daily bread. They owed him a large amount of money, and on the following day it must be paid. "Let him come!" exclaimed their friend; "he shall have it all." At the same moment he said to himself, "I wish my knapsack was filled with the covetous squire's gold."

They now sat down to the scanty meal which had in the mean time been prepared by the girl, who could not help wondering how they would be able to pay the debts which had long been resting heavily upon their minds. At length they arose, whereupon the soldier placed his knapsack on the table and loosened the straps. The old shirt and the stockings without heels rolled out when he opened it, and the space beneath them was filled with more gold and silver than the king had ever had, at any one time, in his treasury.

"Hoorah!" shouted the soldier. "Let him come; he will open his eyes when he sees the gold and silver, and yet he will not dream that he is paid with his own money." The women now took what they needed, the rest was stowed away in a drawer, and the young man went to town for the purpose of buying some new clothes for himself, as he desired to be married as soon as possible to the girl who had been waiting patiently for him all the long eight years.

When he arrived in town he walked into a very fine inn where the wealthy citizens were accustomed to refresh themselves by good eating and drinking. Without paying attention to the curious glances and smiles which were directed towards him, he walked into the large dining-room, sat down at the table, and called the landlord, whom he asked to bring him a good dinner.

"People of your kind had better go into the kitchen," answered the landlord, haughtily.

"Never mind," said the soldier again, "this is good enough for me. Of course, I am accustomed to eat at a better table, but that does not matter, as I am hungry. Bring me a dozen snipes and two bottles of your best wine, and be quick !"

The landlord opened his eyes in wonder ; such a soldier he had never seen before. With remarkable haste the table was laid, and our friend lost no time in satisfying his hunger. He took care to leave a great deal on his plate, as he knew that wealthy and important people usually do this. As soon as he arose from the table, the landlord presented his bill. "Oh," said the soldier, "I nearly forgot to pay you, my friend. Take this; I hope it is enough." At the sight of two shining gold pieces the landlord bowed three times almost to the floor, and expressed the hope that everything had been satisfactory to his excellency.

"Fairly well, fairly well, my good man," answered the soldier, drawing himself up with much importance. Upon this the landlord bowed again, and asked if his excellency desired anything more.

"Yes," said the soldier, "let me have a room for the night."

He was informed, however, with many excuses, that every room was occupied, with the exception of one which could not be used.

"Why not?" inquired he.

"All who have slept in that room," explained the landlord, "were found dead the next morning."

"That is the very room for me!" exclaimed the soldier. "Make it ready."

In spite of all objections. he persisted in occupying the haunted room, so when night came on, and he had finished his business, he bid good-night and retired. As soon as the door was closed behind him, he turned the key in the lock, unstrapped his faithful knapsack and placed it in a corner. Then he seated himself on a chair, prepared for whatever might come.

In a little while there was a noise in the chimney, and a black ball came suddenly rolling through he fireplace and into the room, where it unfolded itself into a black, long-haired devil with two horns and a tail, a long nose, and finger-nails which had lengthened into claws.

"Halloo! Is there more of that kind?" ejaculated the soldier, nodding at the tall black figure.

A fresh hubbub was heard, followed by the appearance of two other devils, the one uglier than the other, and both more hideous than the first.

"Be seated," said the soldier, pointing to three chairs, "and make yourselves at home." The three devils followed the invitation, but soon they began to approach him. One reached for his nose, another began to pull his ears with his claws, and the third grasped him by the throat As he considered this rather forward in them, he cried, "In the knapsack with all of you!" Whether they would or not, they were obliged to creep into the narrow space, and soon only a faint cracking and hissing was heard from within.

"You might have behaved better," said the soldier, talking into the corner where he had thrown his knapsack "But now you will please tell me why you always haunt this room at night."

They answered that it was because there was standing a large pot under the oven filled with old gold coin.

"Very well," said the soldier again ; "I will see that you do not come here in the future, disturbing and even killing blameless people in their sleep." Upon this he undressed and went to bed.

Next morning the landlord came and knocked at the door. As the soldier did not answer, he glanced through the key-hole and saw him lying in bed, quiet and immovable. Thinking that he had suffered the same fate as all others who had slept in this room,

"EVIL-SMELLING POWDER FELL OUT"

the landlord cried for help, and tried to force the door open with his broad shoulders. The soldier, who was awakened by this noise, called and asked what had happened.

"Gracious!" exclaimed the stout landlord, panting for breath, "are you alive yet?"

"Go away from the door!" shouted the young man. "How dare you disturb me with such nonsense?"

"I thought—" began the landlord.

"Leave me alone!" roared the soldier. "If you do not go away I will break every bone in your body." On hearing this the landlord fled in terror.

Later in the morning our friend arose. After breakfast he asked for a blacksmith who could beat the dust out of his knapsack. "I have walked so long with it on my back," said he, "that it has become very dusty. It needs a good beating."

Two strong men were now ordered to carry the knapsack to the blacksmith's shop. In the beginning they wondered why one could not do this alone, but soon they found that their burden became as heavy as four bushels of wheat, and they were wellnigh exhausted when at length they reached their destination. The landlord could not think but that the soldier had lost his wits, so he took the blacksmith aside, and told him to order three of his strongest men to beat the dust out of the knapsack with their largest hammers. The blacksmith gave orders according to these instructions, but no sooner had the dusting begun than such a yelling and shouting was heard that every one thought the world had come to its end. "Don't mind that," said the soldier, "but knock as hard as you can." The men complied, but the knapsack did not seem to suffer the least by their mad hammering.

At length the soldier bid them stop, and asked the two strong men to go and empty the dust into the sea. His order was obeyed, and when the knapsack was opened a large pile of a black, evil-smelling powder fell out. It was the bodies of the three devils which had been beaten into dust.

When the soldier had paid the men well for their services, he accompanied the landlord back to the inn, telling him all that had happened. As soon as the oven was torn down the money came to light. One-half of it was the soldier's share.

Our friend now built a fine little house near the city, was married to his sweetheart, and had enough as long as he lived. The old knapsack followed him everywhere, obtaining for him all that he wished.

But he and his wife always thought their success might be due to the grace and the goodness of God even more than to the old knapsack.

WHEN our first parents were expelled from Paradise they went out among the mountains, and all was darkness around them. "No pity, no hope!" said they to each other. "Without a joy, without the grace of God, we must pass through life, and all who come after us will suffer for our sake, deprived of every joy, every hope, and every bright prospect."

The day began to dawn. As far as could be seen there was only the hard stone. No green grass, no tree, no flower, nowhere a hope! The two lonely beings at the barren rock bent their heads and wept. But far above them, on the summit of the mountain, an angel witnessed their grief. God had expelled them from Paradise, but He loved them still; therefore He bade this angel follow them whither they went.

When the man and the woman felt most desolate and subdued by remorse, he descended from the lofty height where he was seated, and touched the cold stone with his sceptre; and at this same moment life began to grow among the cold stones.

The grass worked its soft and beautiful carpet into the surface of the cliff ; thousands of green shoots emerged from among the stones ; trees forced their roots into the crevices, shading a rippling spring which murmured softly in the deep silence, and everywhere did a little smiling flower-face peep forth from among the beautiful foliage.

When the sun arose, the angel appeared before the man and the woman, and said to them : " This place will be sacred for all time to come, as a memory of Paradise and its glory. Every man and woman shall know of it, and from here they will carry with them into the world bright hopes and memories which cannot fade or be forgotten, however long they may live."

Thus speaking, the angel lifted his wings and disappeared within the deep blue of the sky. But his words were true, and it happened as he said. We all know the beautiful garden among the desolate mountains. There the sweetest hopes are cherished. The best wishes, the brightest thoughts, the purest and friendliest acts are those from **the *Garden of Childhood.***

THE MAN WITHOUT A HEART

HERE was once a wise man. His knowl-
edge was so profound that he might have
invented powder or discovered America
if he had cared to, for neither was known
in his day. His thoughts were, however, far from
the welfare of others, and all that he cared about
was to be left alone with his studies, by which
means he hoped to gain perfect happiness. He
was well aware that Fortune was neither a bag of
money nor good eating and drink'ng. By his ardent and diligent studies he had discovered that
Fortune was, indeed, a great power of nature, like
lightning or magnetism, and he declared that it
should be his one day or another.

Early and late he pursued his studies in nature,
and in old, curious books, with which his rooms
were filled. But he was often disturbed by persons
who wished to consult him on important n.atters,
and who sought his help. As he was wealthy a
great many poor persons came to his door, asking
for a kind word and a penny. He could spare
neither, however. Whenever a poor widow or

motherless child called him away from his books for a short while, he was annoyed. On one occasion, when he was obliged to follow his father's body to its last resting-place, he said to himself, sighing deeply, " I wish I had no heart," thinking if he had none it would be an easy matter to seclude himself from the large world, and his fellow-men, whom he did not love.

When at home, this wise man was, as a rule, occupied with boiling, melting, and mixing the most remarkable things. One day he placed a small pot on a quaint-looking little oven, and was in the act of carrying out a very important experiment. The pot contained, namely : three drops of rat's blood ; forty drops of the juice of henbane and chelidonia ; the finger of a thief, who had been hanged on the gallows ; four slugs ; the heart of a frog, and a bit of his own finger-nail. As soon as this began to boil, the wise man poured three drops of a green fluid into the pot. Instantly a white steam arose, spread itself above the stove, and assumed the shape of a ghost's figure, surmounted by a large head with a pale, colorless countenance, large, round eyes, and a broad mouth.

The old sage was struck with astonishment, and wondered if this figure might, indeed, be Fortune itself.

" What do you wish for ?" asked the figure, with its broad mouth.

"What do I wish for?" repeated the student. "Perfect happiness. Fortune herself is my desire."

"Explain what you mean by Fortune," pursued the spirit.

"Fortune," began the other, "is a power of nature, and—"

"Be quick!" cried the ghost. "Do you wish for money?"

"No, no," answered the wise man ; "the greatest happiness is to have no heart. I wish that you would take mine from me."

"Shall I take your heart?" asked the spirit again.

"Yes, take it, and hide it so well that it will never be found."

"Far, far away," said the spirit, "in the middle of a wild forest, there is a sea with an island on which an old castle is standing. I shall bury your heart fifty feet under the deepest cellar in this castle. Are you contented?"

"Yes, and I shall rejoice to be rid of it."

Now the steam vanished, and the pot boiled quietly as before. The wise man felt a cold touch at the left side of his chest, and knew that he had lost his heart. Since that day he lived much more peacefully, and was able to see the greatest want and distress without feeling the least trouble. He thought himself happier than all other beings, and was able to pursue his studies undisturbed.

In the same country there lived a king who had two sons. These were ready to marry, and the youngest of them was especially urged by the king to seek a wife, as his father was advanced in age, and he was to be his successor. It was decided that the two young men should go into the wide world and seek their wives in the neighboring countries. At length the youngest went away alone, as the king wished to keep one of them to assist him in his duties, of which we know all kings have a great deal.

So the young prince left home, and walked far away, until he reached a house in a large forest, where the wise man without a heart lived undisturbed. It was towards evening, so he knocked at the door and asked the old philosopher, who was by this time over a hundred years old, to give him a bed for the night. He also told him that he was a prince and accustomed to have his will. The old man reluctantly bid him enter, and his surprise may be imagined when he found himself in a spacious study filled with the queerest treasures and specimens that had ever met his glance. He turned to his old host, inquiring, " Do you live here quite alone ?" " Yes," was the answer ; "there is no one but myself living inside these walls, and I care for no companions."

The prince seated himself in a comfortable chair, and continued : " But where are your wife and children ? How can you live without them ?"

" I have never married," replied the wise man, smiling grimly, "and I never shall. My time is too valuable to be spent in the careless world, which seems to live only for idle pleasures and trifling pursuits. I live for a grand purpose."

"Poor man!" said the prince; "you have never been happy. Does it not please you to hear the birds twitter and to feel the warm sunshine? Do you never enjoy the pleasant and solemn sound of church-bells every morning at sunrise, and again at sunset, when the shadows are lengthening over the fields? Do you never feel the blessings of living for others?" "I have thought and studied for many years," replied the philosopher, "but perfectly happy I never was until I lost my heart. I have lost that, and do not wish to have it back." "Poor man!" said the prince again; "what a life to lead! The greatest happiness on earth which I can think of is to have a kind and beautiful wife, and at present I am seeking one. Shall I not try to find one for you also?" "Yes," suddenly exclaimed the wise man, "you may do so." He thought that it might be an advantage to have a young woman in the house to wait on him, as thus a great deal of time might be saved to him. "I shall do my best," returned the prince.

The next morning he pursued his way, and in due time arrived at a kingdom where there were two fair princesses, whom every one, even their enemies, praised. The young man told the king who he was, and that he would like to marry the youngest, and that her sister would be a fit wife for his brother.

The king at once consented, so the three young people entered a carriage and drove away to the home of the prince, who was much pleased with the outcome of his mission.

When they passed the forest where the old hermit lived, they alighted to pay him a visit. As they approached he was standing outside his door, engaged in measuring the distance to the sun with a long pole. Seeing the prince and his two fair companions, he nodded at them, and asked the young man which of the girls was his betrothed. The prince pointed to the youngest, whereupon the philosopher turned to her sister and asked if she was the woman whom the prince had promised to bring him.

"She is to be married to my brother," answered the prince, as the girl was too much afraid to make any reply.

"So this is the manner in which a prince keeps his word!" cried the old man. "If you do not allow me to keep this girl, you will regret it."

"I saw no woman who would be a fit wife for you," returned the prince. "This one is too young."

"You have broken your word!" shouted the wise man; "but I will punish you." Drawing a small staff from his belt, he touched the youngest princess and the prince, converting them into stones with a human shape, but cold and dead. Upon this he seized the other princess by the hand and led her into his house, where he forced her to cook, and wash, and scrub from morning to night, while he sat in his study, occupied with his learned duties. The poor girl never ceased to weep over her hard fate, and often begged him to show mercy; but he paid no attention to her tears and prayers, and merely bid her do her work if she did not wish to suffer the same treatment as the two who were standing immovable outside the house.

As the young prince did not return, the king began to fear that something had happened to him, and asked his eldest son to go and find him. The young man readily complied, and at once set out on his journey. He walked a long distance, until he lost his way in a forest where there was neither path nor road. One afternoon he caught sight of a huge eagle, which sat on a tree, watching the ground beneath.

"Can you tell me," said the prince to the bird, "where to—"

"Wait a moment!" interrupted the eagle. "There is a mole which is about to come up through yonder mole-cast. I wish to have it for supper, as I have seen no birds the whole day."

"Leave the poor fellow alone," said the prince, "and eat this sausage instead. It will give you less trouble, and, besides, the mole is a very useful animal which should be guarded carefully from every danger."

"Many thanks!" returned the bird, seizing the sausage with his sharp claws. "No doubt you are right in regard to the mole, but I am fearfully hungry, so I am obliged to take my chances."

At the same time the mole thrust his nose through the surface of the ground, and said : "Young man, if you are ever in need, call me and I will help you, as you have saved my life."

"Thank you for that promise," returned the prince.

"I will make you the same promise," now resumed the eagle, "because you gave me what you might yourself have needed. But why do you roam about in this forest ?"

The prince thanked him many times, and told him that he was seeking his brother, who had disappeared while seeking a bride.

"I know it," explained the bird. "I saw him from far above ; but it will be difficult to free him from the magician's hands into which he has fallen." And now he proceeded to tell the young man of his brother's cruel fate. "If we could only find the heart of the old philosopher," he said, musingly, "all would be well. Wait! Seat yourself on my back, and we may succeed." The prince obeyed, and was carried swiftly through the air, until the eagle landed on the island in the middle of the forest, where the spirit had buried the magician's heart fifty feet under the deepest cellar of the old castle. "Now call the mole," bade the eagle. The prince obeyed, and at once the small animal thrust his nose into the air, inquiring what he desired.

"Bring us the heart which is buried deep in the
ground below the old castle," said the eagle. The
little fellow at once dug himself into the ground,
and returned, pushing a small gray lump in front of
him.

"Take this lump," said the eagle, "and when we
arrive at the philosopher's house, walk in and bid
him set your brother and the two princesses free.
If he tries to hurt you, throw his heart at him, and
he will obey you."

The prince again seated himself on the eagle's
back, and away they went to the house in the
forest, where the wise old man had so cruelly
treated his brother and the two princesses. Here
the bird stopped his flight, and the prince hastily
entered the house. He saw the philosopher bending over his books and papers, while the princess
was engaged in drying some evil-smelling herbs on
the stove.

"Undo the wrong," cried the prince, "and set my
brother and the two princesses free!"

The old man turned furiously upon him, and
reached for his staff, but at the same moment he
felt a stinging pain in his left side, threw up his
hands, staggered to his feet, and cried: "Mercy,
mercy! I have served the Evil One! Some one
gave me back my heart. Oh, give me my youth
again, that I may live like other men!"

In the next second the two figures outside the
windows became alive again, and the two brothers

clasped each other in their arms, while the sisters held each other by the hand. But a great change had taken place in the room. There now stood by the philosopher's chair a little boy, gazing curiously at the many singular objects about him. This man had found his heart again, and was to begin life afresh.

For none of God's creatures can live without a heart.

JAMES, THE HUNTSMAN

N old man died, leaving behind him two sons. Their only heritage was an old thatched hut, with a small vegetable garden. A table, an old chest, and three or four chairs were all the hut contained.

"Our father has left us but little," said the oldest of the two brothers. As the other said nothing, but merely shook his head, he added : "There is hardly enough to divide between two."

"We might draw cuts," suggested the younger.

"That is hardly worth while," replied his brother. "I would better take it, since I am the oldest."

"You may do so," returned the younger.

"Very well, and you may seek a place in the world for yourself, as best you can. Since we are talking about it, you may as well go at once," continued the older.

So the younger brother departed. His name was James, and of him this story treats.

Having bid his brother farewell, he walked on until nightfall, when he lay down on the slope of a hill, resting his head upon his knapsack. He looked at the clouds, with their beautiful golden tinge, the blue sky, and the silver-gray rye-fields, and thought of the future and of what he would like to be in the world. He had often wished to become a huntsman, but how could he ever obtain the necessary equipment—a shot-gun, a horse, and a horn? While these thoughts came and went, he fell asleep, but was awakened by hearing himself addressed in a feeble voice which sounded near his ear : " Help me, help me !" He arose and looked around, but saw nothing. " Help me !" said the voice again, and this time it seemed to come from the ground beneath his feet. James bent down and examined the grass, where he saw the figure of a dwarf with a large head and thin legs, hardly taller than the finger of an ordinary man or woman.

" Help me, help me !" cried the little man again.

" What ails you ?" inquired James.

" Listen !" said the dwarf. " I live in this hill. To-night I visited my grandfather, who lives in the hill opposite. When I returned, a cow had placed herself over the doorway, and I cannot pass her. Will you chase her away ?"

" Let me look at you a moment !" said James. " I never saw such a little fellow before."

" Yes, but be quick, for if the sun shines on me, I shall be converted into cobweb and night's dew !"

James walked around to the other side of the hill and chased the cow away. " Come back to-morrow night at twelve, that we may reward you," said the dwarf, whereupon he skipped through a small opening, and disappeared in the ground.

The next evening James was standing at the foot of the hill, when suddenly the latter was raised on four red pillars, forming a portal under which the dwarf of the previous evening was standing. "Come in," said he to the young man. "My father will allow you to make three wishes, all of which we shall fulfil."

Without fear James accepted the invitation, and as soon as he had entered the portal, the hill closed above him, whereupon he was led from one magnificent room into another. Thousands of dwarfs were busily engaged in many different occupations, such as sword-making, weaving, and cutting precious stones, and from every corner curious and costly diamonds sent their sparkling rays into space. "Have you decided what wishes to make?" asked the little man. "Yes," replied James. "I want a shot-gun, a horse, and a horn." "You shall have them," said the dwarf, leading him into a room filled with all that belongs to a hunter's equipment. There were guns as large as trees and as small as pen-holders, some plain, some costly, some made of iron and steel, and some glittering with silver and gold and costly stones, such as we never see among us. James looked around, and finally reached for an old, rusty musket, hanging on the wall in a broad leathern strap. "This one will suit me best," said he. "All the fine fire-arms, mounted in gold

and silver, I cannot use, but this one suits me."
"Take it," said the dwarf, smilingly, "and keep it."

In another room they saw a great many beautiful
horns. James looked around, trying to make a
choice. At last he seized a plain-looking bugle-
horn which some one had thrown into a corner.
"All the others will do for kings and knights," said
he, "but this one will suit me." The dwarf told
him it was his, and added, "Now we will go into
the stables and find a horse for you."

The stables were filled with the choicest horses of
all kinds, from the fabled three-legged horse which
walks past the windows at night, when some one is
to die, to the charger which helps the soldier slay
the enemies of his land. Near the door, James
caught sight of a small gray steed, rumpled and
badly kept; he pointed to this horse, saying, "I
choose this little one; he matches the gun and the
horn and me." The dwarf confirmed his choice,
and in the next second James was standing outside
the hill, with his rusty musket, his dented horn, and
the little gray horse. He jumped into the saddle
and rode straight to the king's court, where a sentry inquired about his errand. "I wish to become
one of the royal hunters," said James. "Then you
had better apply to the king's adjutant. If he has
any use for you, he may engage your service," returned the sentry.

So James rode along an avenue shaded by tall
chestnut-trees, and leading to the gateway of the

palace. When he had about reached the latter, a little gray bird which was perched in one of the trees began to sing so beautifully that he involuntarily stopped and listened. The bird flew down, seated itself on the pommel of James's saddle, and began speaking. "Listen to my words! When you sound your horn every one must dance after it, and every one at whom you point with your musket must die. When you see the king, tell him that you will try to free his daughter from the king of the dwarfs, who seized her many years ago, and carried her into the same hill where you were a short time ago; but use your own judgment regarding the way in which to break the might of the dwarf-king. He is cunning. A young prince to whom the princess was to be married is also in his hands. But if you can set these two persons free, and gladden the king's heart, you will become a great hunter, and more."

James was much astonished to hear the bird speak in this manner, and when the little feathered singer left him and swung itself high into the air, he rode into the court-yard, where he was met by the king's adjutant, who asked what he wished. "I desire to become one of the king's hunters," replied James. The adjutant smiled and called several men who were sitting around a table under a large oak-tree, drinking and discussing, as it seemed, very important matters. They gathered about James and the adjutant, and the latter said,

"Here you see a young man who wishes to become one of you!"

"He looks well enough," remarked one of the men. "See his gun! I am sure that barrel was made of the purest gold."

"His horn beats ours!" cried another, winking at his comrades; "it was no doubt cut from one large diamond."

"But his horse!" added a tall hunter. "I verily believe that it served Alexander Magnus when he travelled from India across the ocean to America."

The men laughed uproariously at these jokes, and the adjutant especially had great difficulty in recovering his breath. He was purple in the face from laughing, when he said: "The king had better see him; he has but little amusement since the loss of his children. One of you may go and call him down."

When the king came into the court-yard and saw James and his equipment, he asked, gravely, what he could do for him.

"I wish to become your majesty's huntsman," answered James, "and also to try and rescue the princess and her betrothed husband from the dwarf-king's might. If your majesty will follow me alone, we may depart at once."

"Do you know what you promise?" asked the king. "Six years have passed since these young persons were spirited off into the mountains, and

I have no hope of seeing them again. How will you rescue them?"

"Your majesty shall see," replied the young man. "Follow me to the hill, and let us lose no time. Every second may be valuable."

"If you can save my children," said the king, again, "I will make you my prime-minister, and grant you one-fourth of my kingdom. As you look good and true, I will also follow you. Saddle my horse," continued he, turning to his servants, "and quickly."

Late in the evening James and the king arrived at the foot of the hill which the young man knew so well. "Now we must call the king of the dwarfs," said he, "and force matters with him if he will not come to terms." Thus saying, he sounded his horn for the first time. When the last tone had died away, a fearful noise came from within the hill, and in the next minute the latter was raised upon four pillars, red as fire, disclosing a hall, from the background of which a fearful-looking troll came forward. His body was that of a child, but he had a very large head, with a nose like an old-fashioned winder, and a couple of eyes like dessert-plates. When he saw James, he began to howl furiously.

"Stop your yelling," said the king, "and bring forth my children whom you spirited away. We have come to rescue them, and we will force you to give them up."

"Hoo, hoo!" shouted the troll. "She is the sweetest nightingale. She sings for me from nightfall to daybreak. Hoo, hoo!"

"If you do not bring my daughter here," cried the king, "we will never leave you until we take your life, you monster!"

"Hoo, hoo-o-o-o!" began the troll, again, but at the same moment James again sounded his horn, blowing a merry tune. The dwarf-king fell upon his face, and began to hop about on the point of his nose with wonderful rapidity. He looked so singular that the king could not help smiling, although he had almost forgotten how during the six years in which he had not seen his daughter.

"Hoo, stop! I am over five hundred years old, and you will kill me if this goes on—hoo-o-o-o, hoo!" shouted the troll.

"Bring my daughter!" roared the king. "Bring her as young and pretty and innocent as she was when I saw her last."

"Yes, yes!" panted the troll. "Stop, stop, stop!"

James stopped, and the dwarf-king rushed into another cave, from which he appeared a moment later with the princess, who ran to her father, and was clasped in his strong arms.

"Where is the prince?" asked James. "Forth with him, if you do not wish to hop about another time."

"He is here no more," replied the troll.

"Here he is," suddenly exclaimed the princess,

"'NOW WE MUST CALL THE KING OF THE DWARFS'"

pointing to the little gray steed, which stood near by, gazing at them.

"Give him back his human shape," commanded James.

"Then give me back the gun and the horn," answered the troll. He received them, when suddenly the horse vanished, and before them stood a young and stately knight. With a fearful crash the hill was closed, but the four happy persons were standing in the open field, the sun rising over their heads.

"I will keep my word," said the king, addressing James. "One-fourth of my country shall be yours, and I will give you a duke's rank and title."

"I am contented with less," replied James. "I have received no education, and would not make a good duke, I am sure."

"Never mind your education," asserted the king. "You can easily fill a duke's place without an education."

"Yes, indeed," said the princess.

"To be sure," added the prince.

Thus James became a duke. But the hunters at the royal palace died of envy, every one.

HERE was once a man and his wife who had three sons. The two oldest were tall, strong boys, who helped their father every day in his work, but the youngest was small and sickly, and as he stayed at home most of the time, hanging about his mother, they called him "Mother's Pet." At last the father died, and not long after the mother was taken sick. When she felt that death was near she called her youngest boy to her bedside, and said, sadly: "What will become of you, Mother's Pet, when I am gone? Your brothers are big enough to help themselves, but you are so small and weak!"

"I shall have no trouble," answered the lad. "You need not be worried about that."

So the mother died and was buried. Now the oldest son took possession of the house, and the second oldest took everything that remained.

"What shall I have?" asked Mother's Pet.

"Well, well," said the eldest. "We forgot you. Let us see—yes, you may have the kneading-trough, though. If you can obtain flour and yeast, you may bake dough-nuts and cakes every day, and live like a king."

So Mother's Pet got the kneading-trough, and nothing else. He was satisfied, however, and possessing himself of his heritage, carried it to the sea, where he launched the trough as a boat and put to sea, intending to try his luck in the wide world. When the wind and waves had tossed him about for several days, at length Mother's Pet arrived at a strange land, where he went ashore, bent upon making headway for the king's residence, where he intended to offer his service. Having walked about for several days, he arrived at his destination and went straight to the king.

"What is your name?" asked the stately monarch.

"My name is Mother's Pet. Will you not engage my service?"

"You don't look able to work," remarked the king. "In fact, you are too small and weak."

"I know I am small," replied the lad, "but doesn't your majesty know that a little one may often do a thing before a big fellow can turn around?"

"There you are right," returned the king. "Let us see—yes, chattering you seem to understand well enough, but very little besides, so we'll put you in among the girls in the kitchen."

"That is a start," said Mother's Pet. 'Of course, I should like a better position and a good salary, but so far I am willing to excuse your majesty."

"I am much obliged to you," answered the king

—"very much, indeed. If the occasion arises, I'll know where to find you."

"All right," said Mother's Pet. "When you want a good prime-minister, or general, or admiral, just notify me, and I'll be ready."

"You are very kind," replied the king, bowing him out, "and I hope you will call on me for anything you need."

So Mother's Pet entered the service of the king.

Now this monarch had a very pretty daughter. She was, of course, sought by a great many suitors; in fact, princes and dukes and noblemen swarmed about her like insects about a light.

The princess was sorely troubled about this, as she cared little or nothing for these men who did nothing but idle away their time for her sake, leaving her alone not a single moment of the day, although she tried all possible means to avoid them. One day she came into the kitchen and told the girls of her troubles. None of them understood her, however, as they all considered it pleasant to have a large number of suitors, and would be happy to marry a prince or a duke, or some great nobleman. The only person about the kitchen who sympathized with the princess was Mother's Pet. He happened to recollect an old story that his mother had once told him, and this he decided to use for the purpose of assisting the young lady to get rid of the many suitors surrounding her court.

The princess became greatly surprised when the

lad beckoned her to follow him into the pantry. She complied, however, and when Mother's Pet had closed the door after them he said to her: "Shall I tell you how to get rid of your suitors?" "I wish you would," replied the sweet princess. "Listen," pursued Mother's Pet, "and mark my words! Tell them you are willing to marry any one of them who brings you a hen which lays golden eggs, a golden hand-mill which grinds by itself, and a golden lantern which can light up the whole kingdom."

On hearing this the princess became much pleased; she thanked the boy for his good advice, and afterwards she told her suitors what she expected them to do before she could ever think of giving to any of them her hand in marriage. When a week had passed, every prince, duke, and count had left the palace.

A year passed, but the princess was by no means as merry as of old, and the king, her father, began to feel vexed with the girl, who seemed determined to become an old maid. One day he called her and inquired who had advised her in regard to the hen, the mill, and the lantern. She told him of the boy in the kitchen, who had advised her so well. Upon this her father called him into his presence, and said that if he could not himself procure the three treasures he would be hanged by the neck until he was dead.

"Will I be allowed to marry the princess if I find them?" asked the boy.

"I can safely promise you that," replied the king.

Now the story that the boy remembered was about a troll who lived far away, hundreds of leagues beyond the sea, and who possessed three costly treasures—those, in fact, which he had mentioned to the princess. So he hastened to the beach and put to sea in his kneading-trough.

Having completed his voyage he stepped ashore, and repaired to the house where the troll and his wife were living. As soon as it became dark he mounted the roof of the house and opened a trap-door through which he descended. On the collar-beam the magic hen was perched, so the boy, who knew that caution was necessary, stole silently up to her from behind, and managed to throw his cap over her. But the hen made such a violent effort to gain its liberty, and bragged so loudly, that the troll awoke. The boy climbed down and ran to his boat. The troll, running after him, reached the beach, but the boy was already far out to sea when he reached the water's edge.

"Did you steal my hen?" cried the troll.

"Yes, I did," returned Mother's Pet.

"Will you return?"

"Depend upon it."

"Then I shall catch you," shouted the troll, "and eat you up!"

The king and the princess were well pleased with the wonderful hen with which the boy re-

"BOTH KNELT DOWN AND DRANK"

turned. Mother's Pet was at once made a baronet.

But in a few days he decided to return for the hand-mill and the lantern.

Having reached the troll's house safe and sound, he hid among the trees in the garden until midnight, when he again ascended to the house armed with a heavy club. When he opened the trap-door he could hear the troll and his wife snoring so loudly that every door and window rattled. Now Mother's Pet reached through the opening with his club, and let it fall exactly on the troll's large nose. He awoke immediately, kicked his wife far out on the floor, and asked what she meant by breaking his nasal bone. The woman protested, but in vain; her husband insisted that she had intended to murder him. They very soon came to blows, and while they tumbled out of the door to fight, Mother's Pet stole through the opening, seized the hand-mill and the lantern, which stood on a table near the bed, rushed out of the door, and made for his boat with all possible speed.

The troll's wife noticed the light which issued from the golden lantern, and shouted to her husband, who was beating her violently with the heavy club, "You had better look after our treasures! Some one is running away with them!" They both pursued the boy, but he had already reached his kneading-trough, and was far from the shore when they reached it.

"Are you called Mother's Pet?" cried the troll.

"Yes, I am," was the answer.

"Did you steal my golden hand-mill and my precious lantern?"

"Sure."

"Did you also steal my hen?"

"Who else could it be?"

"Will you return?"

"Yes, when the sea becomes a mountain!" shouted the boy, merrily.

"Let us empty the sea," proposed the woman. Both knelt down, and drank with all their might until they became as thick and firm as a pair of drums. As the water in the sea rushed into their mouths with wonderful rapidity the waves rose as high as mountains, and in spite of every effort on his part the boy's trough rapidly approached the troll's mouth. But at the very moment when his large hand was stretched out to seize the frail boat both he and his wife burst. The water ran back into its cradle with such force that Mother's Pet, the trough, the hand-mill, and the lantern were pushed ashore on the other side, where the king and the princess stood watching for them. They all arrived safely, however, and there was a great joy throughout the land when the princess and Mother's Pet were married.

Mother's Pet became in time a great king. All his subjects were happy, for as the hen laid a golden egg every day there were no taxes to pay, and as the hand-mill provided for every one, all were well supplied with the necessities of life. The golden lantern provided so well for enlightenment that no more schools were needed, and this was the very best of it all—said the children !

HERE were once a man and his wife who had three daughters, Karèn, Marèn and Metté. They were all fine-looking girls, but wicked and ill-natured in disposition, and Metté was the worst and most disagreeable of all. In the course of time suitors came for Karèn and Marèn ; but many days passed before any one ventured to woo Metté. At length, however, a suitor arrived, coming of course from far away. Three times the marriage was to be announced from the church pulpit, and on the third day after the last announcement, at such and such a time, the ceremony was to be performed ; this was his wish.

On the appointed day the man and his wife went with their daughter to the church, but they were obliged to wait a long time for the bridegroom. Finally he made his appearance, riding on an old gray horse, with a rifle across his back, and a pair of large mittens on his hands. A big dog followed him. As soon as the marriage ceremony was over, he said to his wife : " Get up on the horse in front

of me, and let us ride home." So they rode away.
After a while the man dropped one of his mittens.
"Pick it up," said he to his dog. But the dog did
not obey him. "Pick it up at once," he again commanded ; but, no, the dog would not touch it. When
for the third time he had given the same command,
and the dog refused to obey, he seized his rifle and
shot the animal dead. They now proceeded on their
way and soon came to a forest. Here the man desired to rest, so they alighted and turned the horse
loose in the grass. When they wished to proceed
on their journey, the man called to the horse and
twice repeated his call, but all in vain. The animal
paid no attention to him, and seemed determined to
continue enjoying the fine grass under the trees.
Whereupon he again snatched his rifle and shot the
poor creature.

His wife, who witnessed this act, became greatly
frightened, and promised herself that she would
never gainsay her husband. The man now took a
green bough, bent its ends together and gave it to
his wife, saying : " Keep this bough until I ask for
it." They then walked home together.

For several years this couple lived happily, Metté
never forgetting the promise which she made herself in the forest. She was so kind and complaisant, that no one would ever recognize in her "the
wicked Metté." One day her husband said to her :
" Would you not like to go and see your parents ?"
Metté answered that it would afford her great pleas-

ure to pay a visit at her home. Carriage and horses were immediately ordered ready for the journey, and they soon drove off. On the way they noticed a large number of storks. "What nice ravens!" said the man. "They are not ravens; they are storks," said his wife. "Turn back and drive straight home!" shouted the man to his coachman, and back they went to the place from which they came.

Some time thereafter the man again asked his wife if she would like to visit her parents, and she answered that it would please her very much to go. On the road they met a flock of sheep and lambs. "What a number of wolves!" exclaimed the man. "No," returned his wife, "they are lambs and sheep." "Turn back!" said her husband, and back they went a second time.

When some time had elapsed the man again asked his wife if she did not desire to see how her parents were, and she at once consented. When they were fairly started, they noticed some hens. "Look at those crows!" exclaimed he. "Yes, indeed," assented his wife. They proceeded on their journey, and were eagerly welcomed by Metté's parents. Karèn and Marèn were also there, with their husbands. The old mother retired with her daughters to inquire how Metté was living. In the mean time the father filled a mug with silver and gold coin, telling the three men that he whose wife was the most ready to fulfil his wishes would get the money. The first one immediately began to call:

" Karèn, Karèn, come here !" But she did not obey, and even when he opened the door, went in and tried to drag her away, she refused. The second one had no better success with his Marèn. Now the third one's turn came. He walked up to the door and called, " Mettè, come here !" She was immediately before him, asking what he wanted. " Hand me the bough which I gave to you in the forest," said he. She at once produced it, and he, showing it to the two others, said : " Look at this bough ; I bent it while it was green. You should have done the same."

CATTLE-DRIVER once undertook to bring a herd of cattle to town, where the animals were to be sold at the market. The way was long and tiresome, and the roads bad, so one evening he resolved upon stopping at an inn to get a good night's rest. He slept well, and before taking leave ate a hearty breakfast of bread and eggs. But as he was about to draw forth his pocket-book for the purpose of paying the sum due the landlord for lodging and meals, the thought struck him that if he made this payment he might run short of money before arriving in town. As such an event was by no means agreeable, he asked the innkeeper to trust him until he returned, in a few days. This favor was readily granted, and so the cattle-driver pursued his way.

Having sold his stock at a good price, on returning home he arrived at the inn, and inquired for his bill, but to his great surprise, the landlord referred him to an immense sheet of paper covered with calculations and numbers: this was the bill, and the amount due was exactly four thousand dollars.

The cattle-driver at first supposed this to be a joke, but the landlord assured him in full earnest that it could not be calculated a cent less. "You ate ten eggs," said he, "and if those had been hatched, there would have been ten chickens. They, too, might have laid eggs and hatched them, and—well, in four years it would all have amounted to four thousand dollars. I am reasonable, and won't carry the calculation beyond the four years."

The poor fellow protested, and said that such a sum was more than he possessed, or could ever earn, but all in vain. He was promptly summoned to appear before the chief judge or magistrate, on the following day, to defend his case if he could.

As he strolled about in the streets of the village late in the afternoon, a man stopped and asked the reason why he looked so crestfallen and dejected.

"Oh," replied the cattle-driver, "it is useless to tell; no one can give me any help."

"Don't be so sure of that," said the stranger; "I am a lawyer, and we men of the law are generally able to assist others in their troubles."

The cattle-driver, thus persuaded, now told the lawyer how the landlord of the inn had dragged him into the court because he was unwilling, and unable, to pay for the ten eggs and their offspring.

"Well," at length said the lawyer, "is that all?"

"Yes, that is all; and bad enough it is."

"Then put your mind to rest," continued he; "I shall appear in the court and settle the matter for you. You may present yourself at the time set for the case, but the judge is obliged to wait one hour for my arrival; such is the law. I am always busy, so don't expect me before the hour is out."

At the fixed time the driver promptly put in appearance, explaining that some one would be there to speak for him. So the judge waited and waited, and finally, when the hour was about out the lawyer hastily entered, panting and wiping his forehead, as though he had almost run himself out of breath.

"Are you the lawyer who has undertaken to speak for this man?" asked the judge—sternly, too, for judges don't like to be kept waiting.

"Certainly I am."

"Why did you not come before?" pursued the magistrate; "do you think we have nothing to do but wait for such persons as you?"

The lawyer humbly begged pardon; he had been detained in his cornfields.

"Cornfields!" cried the judge; "why, the corn is not half ripe yet."

"No," admitted the lawyer; "it is not ripe, but I was sowing. I boiled two bushels of corn this morning, and at noon I expect to sow it, in order that it may be ripe and ready for the harvest next week."

These words called forth a roar of laughter in the court-room, and the landlord said that most likely the lawyer had lost his reason, since he supposed that boiled corn would grow in the field and become ripe in a week's time.

"It is no more remarkable than that chickens can be hatched from boiled eggs," remarked the lawyer, looking straight at the judge.

Now the judge began to understand. He turned around and asked the cattle-driver whether the eggs he had eaten were boiled.

Of course they were.

The result was that the cunning landlord was fined a hundred dollars, fifty of which were paid to the clever lawyer, and fifty to the man whom the landlord had intended to cheat so shamefully.

The cattle-driver merrily returned home, well contented with the result of his journey. He often used to tell his friends of the time when he received five dollars for each boiled egg he had eaten.

ONG time ago three tailors were living at a town called Landery. As times became bad, and grew from bad to worse, as they sometimes will, they considered it folly to let the needles rust in the cloth, and resolved, therefore, to set out for a more prosperous location. All three were married, so each one received from his wife a good-sized knapsack and the best wishes, whereupon they started on their journey. They walked many miles, and finally found themselves in a large forest, where they lost their way. The more eagerly they sought an opening among the trees the more confused were they, and when the knapsacks were empty, the three friends found themselves obliged to feed upon roots and herbs. This mode of living was, of course, very disagreeable to all, so their joy was great when one day they discovered far away among the trees a magnificent castle. Approaching the beautiful building, they soon arrived at the gate and sounded the knocker. As no one made any response to their call, they walked in. All the doors were open, and the three tailors passed from one gorgeous hall into another without seeing a single person until they entered the kitchen, where a white goose was moving about.

On seeing the tailors, the goose came forward, craned her neck, and greeted the men in the manner of geese which are pleased to see each other. The tailors were happy to find, in the absence of men or women, at least a real goose, and became further pleased when she opened a door and showed them a well-filled pantry. Upon this the bird made a fire in the stove, and, as there were no bellows, flapped her wings towards the flames until a good fire was burning. The tailors now prepared a hearty supper, and carried the dishes into the great dining-room, where they seated themselves and ate to their hearts' content. Arising from the table they thanked the goose, which at once began to speak, saying : " Your hunger and thirst are satisfied, now I shall show you a good resting-place for the night." So she led them into a bedroom containing three fine beds. "Here you may sleep safe and sound," said she, "but one promise you owe me in return for what I have done for you. At midnight a beautiful maiden will enter the room and offer you wine and cake, but you are not allowed to touch it, whatever she says." The men promised to obey her, and so she departed, leaving them alone to enjoy a good night's rest.

At midnight they awoke, when a beautiful maiden entered the room with a beaker of wine in one hand and dainty cakes in the other. She offered it to the three men with much kindness, but they all refused, saying they had had enough at the supper-table and needed no more. Realizing that they were determined to receive nothing, the maiden withdrew, and the tailors slept quietly until morning. When they arose, the goose had already prepared their breakfast. She bade them kindly good-morning, saying: "Last night you braved the temptation, so I am in hopes that you may be able to dispel the enchantment that rests upon this castle and the forest all around. When breakfast is over, you may start in search of the sorcery. Somewhere you will pass, however, a tree which carries gold leaves from midnight until noon, but if you wish to free me, you are forbidden to touch them."

The three tailors accordingly left the castle and passed through a fine garden. There stood the tree, gleaming in the morning sunshine with its sparkling golden-red splendor. "Well," cried one of the men, "a fool is he who will go in search of sorcerers when he may become wealthy here without the least danger!" The second tailor thought likewise, and so the two seized upon the leaves, and filled their pockets and knapsacks until these were entirely stuffed with the golden treasure. But the third tailor said to his comrades: "I intend to keep my promise to the goose, and, besides, I should like to see the end of this enchantment. So you may return home if you like, but I shall remain here."

The comrades received these words with laughter and scorn, and said they considered him very foolish. In spite of this he remained firm, and so the two men started for their homes, being fortunate enough to find their way out of the forest.

The third tailor now pursued his way among the trees and bushes until he heard the sound of delicious music, which seemed to come from far away. Following the direction of the sound, he walked on, and finally reached a hill, at the top of which a giant was lying on the bare ground, tied securely with ropes on hands and feet, and unable to make a single movement. A flock of geese were trotting back and forth over his body, and near by sat the young woman who had appeared the previous night, playing a harp.

The giant, turning his head, looked at the tailor, and said: "If you are a Christian seize the club which lies behind my head and knock me dead, for it is a slow death to be trodden down by geese." The tailor did not hesitate, but grasped the club and struck the giant's large head with all his might. At the same moment a great change took place. The geese were transformed into men and women, and the giant arose, active and alive, but quite altered; he was a prince of fair countenance and stately bearing. But the beautiful maiden was changed into an old, ugly-looking witch, which flew far away, never to be seen again. The prince thanked the little tailor most heartily for his brave and noble conduct, while his wife, who had been living at the castle in the shape of a white goose, joined them. "A malicious witch," said she, "had changed us all. Because of your timely help, we now offer you a gift which will be very useful to yourself and your family. Take this table-cloth. When you spread it out, saying, 'Cloth, serve quick!' it will provide you with all you wish to eat or drink." The tailor thanked them for this valuable gift, thinking that he now possessed all that he could wish for, and bade the good people a hearty good-bye.

When he had walked a while and gained sight of the open land outside the forest, he determined to make a trial with the cloth, and spread it out upon the sod, saying, "Cloth, serve quick!" At once a fine array of all his favorite dishes stood before him. He had barely finished his meal, however, when twelve giants rode up, and, seeing the remnants of the feast, asked why he had reserved nothing for them. They were hungry and thirsty, and demanded all they could eat, coaxing and threatening the poor tailor, until he ordered the cloth to bring forth whatever they wanted. This done, the giants fell to eating, and were quite contented with the tailor's quick response to their orders. When they all were satisfied, they inquired about the cloth, which they wanted to buy of him. "Here is a sack,"

said the chief of the twelve ; " when you open it, call-
ing, ' Every one out,' you will have as many soldiers
with swords and cannon under your command as
you wish for, until you call, ' Every one in.'   I am
willing to exchange this sack for your table-cloth."
But no, the tailor did not wish to part with his treasure.   " I care more for having a good meal," said he,
"than for killing people."

On hearing this the giants laughed, and their
chief cried: " You are a great fool !   It would serve
you right if we robbed you of the cloth ; but, as an
honest man, I can't do this.   The sack you shall
have, and we take the table-cloth."   So he threw the
sack down to him, seized the cloth, and the twelve
giants were off.

The tailor was not at all satisfied with this treatment, but after a moment's thought he exclaimed:
" That fellow called himself honest.   Maybe he was
even more silly.   Let us see !"   Opening the sack
he called aloud, " Every one out !" whereat one
soldier after another came forth until there was a
great and formidable army.   Then the tailor ordered them to pursue the giants and return with his
table - cloth.   The soldiers obeyed, overtook the
twelve men, and, after a fearful struggle, succeeded
in slaying them and in recovering the precious
article.   The little man was well pleased; holding
out his sack, he cried, " Every one in !" whereupon the entire army disappeared in the sack.   So
the tailor went home, contented with his good luck

When he arrived at his old house in Landery the door was opened by his wife, who at once asked if he had been as successful as his two comrades, who were now rolling in wealth, and had become so haughty that their wives did not seem to know her at all. But the little tailor could not show her the least gold ; he had found nothing of that kind. So the woman scolded him and said he was a simpleton who did not deserve better than to stand at the doors of his former friends begging for a breadcrumb and a penny. "Well," answered the tailor, "I think I shall go and see if they don't remember me." He went out accordingly and asked the two men, who were now wealthy merchants, if they were not willing to assist him with some of their riches, as he had been less successful than they and returned empty-handed. They answered, however, that this was impossible. If he had watched his opportunity and been as careful of his chances as they were he needed not return home without means. Now it was too late, and—dear them—they must be mindful of their own business.

"Well," said the tailor, "though you refuse to help me I shall at least show you that I remember old comradeship. Come and take dinner with me to-morrow, and let me make a little feast in honor of my safe return." The others wondered at this, but promised to come, silently asking themselves what such a poor devil might have to feast upon.

When the little man returned home, telling his

wife that he had asked the two wealthy merchants to come and dine with them the next day, she clapped her hands in dismay, and said she did not know what to put on the table. Her husband asked her, however, to remain quiet, and keep the room tidy for their guests ; he would himself provide for the table. So on the following day the two men arrived. The tailor had gone out, but his wife told the guests he would return with some bread and butter, and a bottle of something, perhaps. When they had waited a little the tailor arrived with his table-cloth, which he spread out on the table, saying the magic words. Thus he brought forth a number of the most excellent dishes and cakes and wine, such as would satisfy even the most pampered appetite. The woman was much astonished, and the two merchants ate and drank to their hearts' content, entirely forgetting their pride and high station. They wished to learn how he had come into possession of such a treasure, and the tailor told them it was a gift from the white goose. But now they must, he said, drink a glass of wine in honor of his happy return. This they did, but at the same moment there was such a shooting outside that even a king's birthday could not be celebrated with greater honor. The guests were fairly trembling for fear, but the tailor laughed and said that he merely wished them to know how wealthy and noble persons were wont to entertain their friends. A moment later he went outside and bid his soldiers to get back into the sack so no one saw them. In a little while the two guests departed, but near the tailor's door they were met by a royal servant. His majesty had heard the shooting, and wanted to know what it meant. So they told how it had all happened, and what a wonderful table-cloth the tailor possessed. As soon as the king learned this he started for the little man's house, followed by all his noblemen, and asked permission to look at the treasure. The tailor readily complied, and spread out a fine lunch for his majesty and the courtiers. The king was pleased and wished at once to buy the wonderful cloth; he offered the tailor any price, but in vain; the little man refused all offers. Then the king grew angry. "I shall show you, upon my word," cried he, "who I am! If you are obstinate I shall use force against you. Don't you know, man, that a king should have his will?" But the tailor persisted, and so the king rode away, carrying with him the precious table-cloth.

On the following day, when the royal court dined at the castle, every one being in high spirits on account of the glorious meals he was now to receive every day, whether the treasury were filled or empty, a fearful shooting and hubbub was heard outside. The castle had been surrounded by a great army, and some one cried out that unless the table-cloth was surrendered the tailor was determined to kill every one, from the king downward, and not leave behind him as much as a tired crow might perch upon. The king became terribly frightened, and was nearly choked in a fine piece of canary-bird steak; but as he found that defence would be of no use, he forwarded the table-cloth at once, and offered to the tailor, who proved himself such a mighty man, a position as chief commander of the government armies. The offer was accepted, and the tailor liked his new occupation, because he was never himself asked to fight, but able to let his soldiers do the acting. So he lived pleasantly all the rest of his days, and often visited the court, bringing with him the magic table-cloth, which gained for him the good-will and friendship of the king and all others. He died in old age, honored and beloved on account of his fine dinners; and the two other tailors often thought their comrade had taken the wiser course, and gained the greatest happiness.

I think so too.

THE PIKE

HIS story begins on a beautiful, warm summer day, many years ago—a Sunday, moreover. The birds were chirping sweetly in the calm woods; around the edges of the yellow-tinted cornfields shone thousands of many-colored, sweet-scented flowers; in short, everything was peaceful, quiet, and agreeable.

At the outskirts of Timmylimtimtown there lived a fat old monk who had settled in the neighborhood of a small chapel, where the peasants would hold their service on Sunday morning. So the worthy Father Jonas had repaired to the place of meeting on this particular Sunday morning, and the members of his flock arrived, one after another, when Brother Timmy Timmylim, who lived a short distance down the road, appeared, standing at his gate, enjoying the beautiful, fresh morning breeze. The bees hummed merrily; one butterfly after another danced across the road, while Timmy stood leaning on the gate, meditating if he might not spend his Sunday in a more profitable way than sitting in the little, crowded chapel, falling asleep when Brother Jonas arrived at the latter half of the sermon. What if he slipped through the back yard and crept down the hill to the little sparkling brook, where pikes were plentiful? There he might rest comfortably on the grass under the shady alders, and smoke his pipe and watch the pikes going up the stream until one of them swallowed his bait and hook and was caught. Then he would bring the fish into the kitchen and ask his wife to fry it in butter—fresh, yellow, delicious butter. Um-m-m, what a fine gravy that would make!

So Timmy went down to the brook, seated himself comfortably under a big tree, and threw out his line. In a little while there was a great splash in the water, followed by a violent tug on the line. Timmy jumped to his feet and pulled with all his might. At length he brought up a large pike—so large and fat and firm that he did not remember having ever seen the like of it. It did not take long ere the fish was securely fastened to a string and hung on a hook on Timmy's back porch, awaiting its final fate.

In the mean time Father Jonas had preached his sermon in the chapel across the way, and on returning home he decided to stop at Timmylim's to learn the reason why Timmy had not put in appearance.

"How are you, brother?" said he, entering the spacious drawing-room, where Timmy rested in delightful anticipation of the forthcoming dinner.

"How is your good health, my friend? You weren't at the chapel this morning, I believe. Why, I stood there, talking and talking, and, upon my word, every little while I looked around to see if my good friend had not arrived; but then I happened to think how fond Timmy is of — ahem — fishing."

"My land!" cried Timmy, in great astonishment. "How could Father guess that?"

"Well," replied the minister, blinking at the farmer in a mysterious manner, "I don't know. I suppose the fine weather made me think so; and then, it *is* mighty nice pastime to sit under those alders waiting for the fish to bite—I know it is."

"How in all the world did Father learn that?" cried the farmer again. "Now, to speak the truth, I *was* awfully sleepy. I got up very early, and then I thought it would be a shame to fall asleep during the service. So I says to myself, 'Better move about, Timmy,' says I, and so it came that I went down to the brook."

"Oh yes," observed the minister, "yes, of course; you are excused, Timmy. Upon my word, if I were not forced to be punctual, I might not always myself—ahem. I was going to ask whether you caught anything."

"To be sure I did," proudly admitted Timmy. "I caught a mighty big pike. Perhaps Father will be pleased to step out and take a view of it."

Out they went, and the preacher exclaimed:

"What a fine specimen, Timmy! Indeed you were lucky. How firm and solid the meat is! But, my friend," added the worthy man, after a short pause, "it was not what I call right to go fishing on the Lord's day, especially at the very time when the service was held. You know, Timmy, the third commandment, don't you?"

The farmer winced slightly at this mild reproach.

"Father mustn't be angry with me," said he, at length. "Indeed, I was just thinking if it might not be well to keep the fish until to-morrow, and ask Father to come and take dinner with us. Father would do me a great favor by coming."

"Thank you, my friend. I am greatly obliged to you. Indeed, I shall be here."

So they talked a little back and forth about weather and winds and the crop, whereupon the minister took leave and returned home.

Sitting in his cosey arm-chair before the open window, Father Jonas, softly fanned by the mild summer breeze, fell into a day-dream, from which he was aroused when supper-time drew near, and he felt hungry. Reflecting upon the scant provision in the cupboard on the wall, he came to think of Timmylim's pike. Such a fish! What if he had a bite of pike for supper, and what if John, his servant boy, skipped over to the brook and tried his luck? Dear him, how such a fish would taste, with butter-gravy and fried potatoes!

"John!" called Father Jonas, bending forward

and thrusting his head out of the window. "John, let's see you!"

John promptly appeared, asking what his master desired.

"Johnny," said the preacher, "don't you think you might go down to the brook and catch a pike or something for supper? I have been sitting here the whole afternoon, thinking of fish."

"It's too late," replied the boy. "Pikes don't bite in the afternoon."

"Don't they?" exclaimed Father Jonas, greatly astonished. "Why, this morning I saw a large pike hanging at the back porch of Timmy Timmy-lim's house—such a big, fat one, too! Now, Johnny—Johnny, my boy—don't you think—I mean go and try, and do your best, and find something for me. I know I can trust you."

Johnny left with a nod and a knowing smile, and lo! in a little while he returned with a beautiful pike, large and firm and fat.

So Father Jonas had pike, with fried potatoes and butter-gravy, for supper, in spite of the fact that pikes refuse to bite in the afternoon.

Next day he repaired punctually to Timmy Tim-mylim's house.

"Oh, my land!" cried Timmy, in great anguish, when the preacher entered. "What shall I do and what shall I say! The pike is gone—stolen right out of the yard, before my eyes, and yet I did not see the thief."

"Why, that is very disagreeable," meant Jonas; "that is, indeed, very discomforting. But now you see, my friend, that I was right in saying that there was no blessing in that pike. You caught it on a Sabbath day."

"No, indeed, there was no blessing in it," ruefully repeated the farmer. "But couldn't Father read in his books and find out who is the thief?"

The preacher shook his head.

"No," said he, "it cannot be found out. Remember, my friend, it was caught on the Sabbath."

"Such a rascal of a thief," cried Timmy, in great anger, "to steal that fine, fine fish! But won't Father do me the favor of condemning the robber, whoever he may be, from the pulpit next Sunday?"

"That I can," asserted the preacher, "and that I'll gladly do for you."

"It will be such a satisfaction!" said the farmer. "I shall be sure to remember Father with a couple of fat geese for Thanksgiving. Next Sunday Father will see me in church, and I'll be sure to keep awake and listen to Father's speech on the thief. Don't spare him, Father."

"Certainly not, Timmy," answered Jonas. "Leave that to me. That fellow will get exactly what he deserves."

On the following Sunday Timmy Timmylim went early to church. Father Jonas preached with great force against stealing and robbing, and finally mentioned that somewhere in the village there was a scoundrel who had robbed Timmy Timmylim, their friend and brother, of a very valuable article. He considered it fitting and proper to call down divine punishment over the thief, unknown as he was, the congregation having no other means of reaching him. If it were not for a certain reason, known only to himself, he might consult certain books and discover the name of the culprit.

In a tone trembling with zeal and fervor, the preacher concluded thus :

> *" Oh, Heavenly Father, friend divine,*
> *Condemn the one* (softly) who threw the line,
> *And punish him as best you like.*
> (Softly) Oh, bless thou him *who stole the pike!"*

"Amen !" gravely added Timmy Timmylim, from his seat somewere down the aisle, in great emotion.

ONG, long ago there lived in the western part of Jutland a minister and a deacon. There were two congregations and two churches, but the one minister had charge of both.

One Sunday, the minister and his helpmate, the deacon, were driving across the country, when they observed a herd of beautiful cattle in a cornfield next to the road.

"Nice cattle," said the minister.

"Amen," agreed the deacon.

"I wish I were able to buy one of the heifers," continued the reverend gentleman, sighing.

"Indeed!" replied the deacon, and mused a little; but then he continued: "Maybe it could be managed if we went over here to-night—you know."

"Certainly not," said the minister, earnestly; "that would never do."

"It would," persisted the other. "No one would suspect persons in our position."

When midnight came, the two men sneaked along the road and entered the field, where they caught and killed a fine-looking heifer, and afterwards divided the meat into two parts, one for each of them. They were unable to agree, however, upon the question of who should receive the hide, but finally the deacon proposed that they might wrestle for it. This they did; the minister taking hold at the horns, and the deacon seizing the tail. So they tugged quite a while, until the tail slipped away from the deacon's hands, upon which he tumbled over, receiving a severe bump at the place which is highest when you are gathering acorns. Thus the minister won the hide, and both men returned home with their spoils.

Some time hence the bishop was inspecting the churches and schools of his district, and was, upon his arrival at the parsonage, well received by the pastor and his family. Later, the deacon and several faithful church-members were invited to supper, in honor of the bishop's arrival. During the evening, this eminent gentleman took occasion to utter his pleasure in finding that the minister and the deacon agreed so well in every way.

"Well," observed the deacon, "we do, that is quite true—and yet I remember one occasion when we really did get into a small scramble. It occurred when we went out in the night stealing a heifer. We shared the meat brotherly, but we fought over the hide."

On hearing him proceed in this manner, the clergyman grew pale and arose, asking the deacon to step outside with him. When the door had closed after them, he said : "Are you crazy, man? Don't you know that if the bishop learns all about the matter you told him of, we shall both become unhappy for the rest of our lives?"

"Just let me talk," answered the deacon, smiling. "He sha'n't learn anything. Leave it to me." So they returned to the dining-room.

"Well," said the bishop, "what did you then do with the hide?"

"The hide? Oh yes," replied the deacon. "Yes, we fought over it; and finally I fell, because the tail happened to slip out of my hands—and I got an awful bump, you know—and *then I awoke!*"

"O—oh, was it only a dream?" observed the bishop.

"Of course; yes, of course it was," replied the cunning deacon. "It could be nothing else—nothing else, your Eminence."

THE DEACON'S WIFE

THERE was once a deacon who had the bad luck of being married to a very ill-natured woman. As he was famous for his singing, the church-members of his parish would often invite him to attend weddings and other festivities, which he did. The woman was, however, very seldom included in these invitations, and the deacon grudged, whenever he returned home, to tell her of the good company he enjoyed. At length he grew tired of her angry words and sullen demeanor, and one night, returning from a feast in one of the villages in the neighborhood, he invited two other deacons to step into his house before they went home, as he wished to see if his wife would preserve her disagreeable manners in the presence of strangers.

Upon entering the house the deacons pulled off their caps and greeted the lady civilly. Her husband gave her many good words, and asked her to wait upon their guests. But she seemed possessed of a mute spirit, and never opened her mouth to say a word. The deacon pleaded long in vain, but finally realizing that his guests would not receive from her anything to bite or to drink, he asked them to walk over to a tavern across the way; he would join them there.

When they had departed he once more talked kindly to the woman, reminding her of her duties as a housewife. But she remained mute, and did not even seem to hear what he said. Now the deacon became frightened and thought she had entirely lost her speech. He began to think, and recollected having once heard that cherry-wine was an excellent remedy for this sickness. Such wine was, however, too expensive to be thought of, and, besides, the drug-dealer lived far off. As the woman would not open her mouth, and something must be done ere long, he determined to try the effect of a few supple limbs of a cherry-tree which grew in the yard; but, as she could not swallow the branches, he was obliged to use them in *another manner*, and did so.

The result was indeed wonderful, for, lo and behold! she spoke at once, and raised her voice until every one in the neighborhood realized that she was talking! The mute spirit left her at once, and, better yet, never returned.

Thus the wonderful healing properties of the cherry-tree were first made known. He who told this story added that an ordinary cane or hazel bough would work the same wonder. Any one in want of a remedy against a woman's obstinacy may try their effect.